A. M. KHERBASH
Bed and Breakfast

Copy edited by Claire Rushbrook

ISBN: 979-8-9866695-2-6

www.amkherbash.com

"We cannot see anything until we are possessed with the idea of it, take it into our heads,—and then we can hardly see anything else."
—Henry David Thoreau

"The flesh is the surface of the unknown."
—Victor Hugo

1

"You can remove the blindfold now, honey."

He sounded eager, and perhaps he was. The gesture was eye-rollingly hokey, but all the same Emma went with it. After a stretch of drab months in which she said "No" to movies and dinner dates ("No" to anything that wasn't staying in and dining on ready-made meals or heated leftovers) Emma began to feel guilty—not to the point of forgetting her own grief, but enough to agree to put on the silly blindfold and do things his way for once.

She removed the blindfold, squinting against the flash of late afternoon sun streaming through the car's windshield. Before her stood a white, two-story house, tall and solid amidst the fluttering spray of autumn leaves. Emma turned to her husband, Nolan, who sat next to her in the driver's seat, meeting her gaze with a boyish smile.

"Why are we here?" she asked.

"I booked us two nights here," he said. "You know, for the weekend."

Emma uttered a small sound, meaning to say something yet failing to find the words. Nolan, perhaps taking her non-answer as evidence of a lagging memory, pointed to the hanging sign that spelled out the property's name.

"Tappy West Creek Bed & Breakfast," he said, hurrying his glance back to his wife so as not to miss the dawning look of recognition. "We spent a few nights here last year, remember?" His smile faltered when he reached for her hand and found it clutching the fingers of its counterpart.

Quietly she said, "I thought we were going on a picnic or someplace to watch the sunset or something."

"A picnic?" her husband gently scoffed. "Who takes a ninety-minute drive for a picnic?"

"I don't know," she snapped back. "I didn't keep track of time—the blindfold put me to sleep. And I didn't get a chance to pack anything. How am I going to spend the weekend here without a change of clothes?"

"Honey, relax. I packed your bags and everything. It's all taken care of."

"Well—" she began digging around for a counterargument— "maybe I had other plans."

"What other plans? Em, it's been ages since you left the house!"

"Fine," she said, opening the car door abruptly. "Let's just go in. I need to use the bathroom."

Nolan waited for Emma to slam the car door shut and disappear into the house before resting his head against the top of the steering wheel. Though glad their conversation had progressed beyond the monosyllabic exchange typical of the past few weeks, he let out an exasperated sigh, gave it a moment to dissipate, then fetched a long breath.

The reception area was picture quiet—dim in the transient hour between late afternoon and early evening, when an amber shade steals over every inch of wall and furniture, save for the gleaming edge of glass, the shining curve of wood, and above them the shimmering crystals of a small chandelier that caught the residual light and threw it back in dapples of color.

Nolan stopped at the unmanned front desk and set the overnight bags down between his thin ankles, pushing back his thick frame glasses as he rose up and cast about for a staff member. The lobby's seating area was deserted, and the only faces he found there were the smiling and grimacing countenances of Noh masks.

This was the same bed and breakfast of last year where Nolan and his wife had enjoyed a happy weekend together, and while the experience itself was more memorable to Nolan than the generic cottage interior, he did not remember seeing those mounted heads—nor did he recall the lobby being crowded with an abundance of potted plants. Gone were the painted ceramic vases and display china, replaced by clusters of dark foliage and green vines cascading down their woven nests, so that the ivory figures and wooden carvings lining the fireplace mantle appeared like forest-dwellers huddled under the arching leaves. All this lent a wild, almost unkempt aspect to the lobby in spite of its surface cleanliness; but much like the tang of charred wood that hung in the air, it was not unpleasant.

Nolan strode back to the reception area and was about to ring the service bell when he heard a hushed voice issuing through a door that stood ajar behind the front desk. The whispers were low enough to conceal any identifying qualities, though Nolan caught the harsh sibilations of what sounded like a heated argument. He hesitated, then rang the service bell.

The whispers died out.

"Excuse me," he called out, waiting for a response before giving the bell another polite tap.

No one emerged to answer the summoning, but at length someone spoke from behind the door.

"What do you want?" The voice was deep, set in that ambiguous range between masculine and feminine; its owner remained hidden from view even as Nolan craned his neck to catch a glimpse of the speaker. All he saw beyond the half-closed door was the empty portion of a narrow room, wall to wall carpet, and a bright westward window.

"We made reservations for the weekend," said Nolan, slightly raising his voice to make sure it carried clear.

The individual behind the door seemed to consider this, taking an appreciable amount of time before answering, "We're closed."

Nolan, who had been bending over the desk's high counter for better hearing, straightened at the unexpected answer. "What do you mean closed? I called not ten days ago and booked a room for this weekend. They said it was fine—no one said anything about closing."

"There's been a change in management," said the voice, "so now we are closed. I suggest you find another place."

Nolan surveyed the empty lobby, the vacancy of which he had mistakenly attributed to a slow hour. His gaze passed over a corridor that lead to the a small guest washroom, then went back to leaning over the desk to keep their discourse from traveling down the hallway. "Look—would you please come out to discuss this? I'm sure we can work something out."

"There's nothing to discuss."

"You said there was a change in management. Who's in charge of booking?"

"No one's in charge of booking. No one is here."

"You're here," argued Nolan with outward calm. "Are you the caretaker?"

"I'm the owner," came the curt reply, leaving Nolan at a loss. Confrontation was not in his nature, though the situation taxed his patience and he dreaded having to tell Emma that they drove all the way here for nothing. She might not have been enthusiastic about the trip, but the long drive back would not be a happy one. He pictured her staring out the window, refusing to look at him let alone say anything, her reticence louder than any outburst of anger. Once home, the resentment may subside, but she would sink back into profound sadness, and her state would trebly weigh on him thanks to his failure. The whole point of coming here after all was to recall happy memories and hopefully return home with some fresh ones.

So far Nolan saw no chance of that. And yet—might he not persuade the owner to let him see their old room for a few minutes? Emma loved that room, and perhaps seeing it again, however briefly, might put her in a better humor—more sympathetic to his good intentions. To be sure, she would be disappointed to hear that they won't be staying, but Nolan was banking on leaving with happier reminisces if nothing else, which in his estimate was far better than hauling their overnight bags and announcing to his wife that they're leaving.

"Could we..." Nolan falteringly began, still wavering between asking the owner point-blank and inching towards his request; he was further stalled from speaking when he turned to address the doorway behind the front desk and caught a glimpse of a shadow darting out of sight. The door remained ajar, undisturbed by this motion, leading Nolan as to puzzle over the darting shadow and whether it was the owner spying on him before disappearing, or a mere trick of light. At any rate, he had little time to dwell on the matter, more so when a muffled splash of water issuing from the bathroom down the hall warned him that Emma would soon be back.

"Listen," he began again, leaning a little farther over the desk to let himself be heard without having to raise his voice. "I know you're closed, but would it be possible for us to have a look at the room upstairs—just for a few minutes. See, I planned this whole trip as a surprise for my wife. We spent a weekend here last year, and I meant for us to come here sort of—as an anniversary gift. I even booked the same room— Room Three. I know we can't stay but at least let us have a look. We won't take long—we'll even leave our bags here. I'm just asking for a few minutes. Five minutes, that's all I ask. *Please*."

Nolan clasped his hands to conclude his earnest plea, ignoring the sensation of the desk's edge digging into his ribs. For a while, the only response he received was an enduring silence attended by the diffused glow of a setting sun shining through the westward window. Then he caught a whiff of a loamy, sulfurous odor and began to wonder whether the place was closed for fumigation.

Emma came by and found Nolan almost bent over the front desk with his hands clasped before him—a strange-enough position, though from the startled look of guilt on his face she may as well have caught him smoking in the boy's bathroom at school.

"What's going on?" she asked while her husband disentangled his hands and took a step back, adjusting his glasses with a nervous smile. Before he could answer, a voice spoke from behind the door.

"Five minutes, then. Five minutes is all I'm giving you."

"Five minutes of what?" asked Emma.

Her question went unheeded as Nolan profusely thanked the disembodied voice, took Emma by the hand and led her upstairs.

2

It occurred to Nolan as they mounted the steps that since the place was closed they may find their room in an altered state, with the walls stripped or covered in tarp, and the furniture wrapped in dust sheets and pushed aside, so it was no small relief when he opened the door and stole a furtive glance about to discover that nothing had changed.

The sight of the room had the hoped-for effect on Emma: even in her morose state she showed signs of wordless delight, entering the room with a roaming gaze and the slow tread of one stepping on hallowed ground. Nolan followed her with less awe, but with a sentimental eye that passed over the plush bed, sheer curtains, and Persian blue wallpaper boasting an ornate pattern of spiraling vines and fat white roses. The interior was not to his taste, though he was beginning to see why Emma was so taken with it—what a far cry it was from dull white walls, grey carpet, and the marred and mismatched furniture of their apartment. Emma had tried to soften the austerity with floral bedsheets, framed prints, and baskets of potpourri, and it presently struck Nolan that since their weekend plans were cancelled, they may as well embark on a project to redecorate their apartment to suit his wife's fancy. Their budget may be limited, but they were free to browse, plan and research, perhaps even try their hand at painting the walls—an undertaking which would surely occupy Emma long enough to draw her out of her melancholy.

Nolan smiled, happy to have hit upon a suitable alternative, and he said to himself that he couldn't care less if Emma spent weeks methodically morphing their whole apartment into an imitation of this room as long as it made her happy. And who knows? She may even find a hobby if not a calling in interior design; she might decide to go back to school to study the art and pursue a more fulfilling career... perhaps, after all, this whole trip was not for nothing, not when he saw light ahead and a path forward.

Nolan continued to stroll through daydreams until his foot kicked something on the floor near the bed. He adjusted his glasses as he looked down only discover an infant doll lying on the lush carpet, half-hidden by the bed skirt. The bald-headed doll stared back with round blue eyes, a puckered mouth, and one plump arm carelessly thrown back. Nolan kicked it under the bed with the promptness of the guilt-stricken, startling Emma who sat on one corner of the bed. She looked up, and her husband caught the glimmer of tears in her eyes.

"Oh, honey," he murmured in sympathy, seating himself beside her.

Emma pressed her lips together and tried to blink away the tears. When she spoke, it was barely above a whisper. "Why did we come here? Why here of all places?"

The question caught Nolan off-guard. He felt himself all at once being pulled in several directions: a part of him was set on bringing up happy memories by way of answering her; another wanted to stay quiet and listen while she spoke; and a third was tempted to seize this opportunity to tell her that they didn't have to stay if she didn't want them to. In the end, he took her hands, made them unclasp the bit of skirt fabric she was clutching, and held them close to him.

"I just thought you'd like it here," he said simply, rubbing his thumb over her fingers. "You've been cooped up for weeks, and I thought the change would do you good." After a pause he added, "I just want you to be happy, Em."

She regarded him with eyebrows gathered in a steeple-like slant over brimming eyes, and at the last line dropped her gaze in a pained frown.

Nolan stared, crestfallen. Even the temporary change was too much for her. He leaned forward and pressed his lips to his wife's furrowed brow in an impulsive kiss. When he drew back, the furrow disappeared, and she was quiet—but it was an encouraging quiet, her brown wet eyes searching his with a trace of surprise and wonder. The air in the room was honeyed with the setting sun. His mind too had gone silent, and his surroundings soon faded as he half-closed his eyes and leaned in.

A knock on the door interrupted his course.

"Oh, go away," he groaned.

"Mr. May?" he heard through the closed door, and all at once remembered the owner, his promise, and the overall time limit imposed on them. Nolan sprang to his feet but took a moment to compose himself before answering the door. Though he expected to find someone there, he nevertheless couldn't help an inward start when he saw the figure standing in the hallway.

"I'd like to speak to you, Mr. May," said the owner in a polite, almost conciliatory tone. There was something jarring about her look, and before the initial jolt had subsided Nolan understood why: her eyelids were weighed down with heavy lashes, dense enough to resemble two black caterpillars. Less dramatic—though no less comical—was the bright lipstick painted over her straight mouth, which had the adverse effect of diminishing her thin lips. Her voice had the deep rasp of a chain-smoker, and about her was the same pungent scent Nolan had detected in the lobby.

"Yes, of course," came the lagging answer from Nolan as he stepped out and closed the door behind him.

"You never told me you were returning guests, Mr. May," the owner resumed, seeming not to notice or mind Nolan's persistent stare. Past her heavy makeup, Nolan estimated she was anywhere north of forty-five or fifty years; she was lean, almost to the point of dryness, her pasty complexion tight and traced with trivial lines; her hair, however, was immaculately dark and thick, and coiled around her head in a crown braid. There was severity in her straight-backed bearing and the black-sleeved arms bent at the elbow to keep one bony hand closed over the other; she appeared more suited to run a grand hotel or some old and stately establishment, but here—in this quaint, out-of-the-way bed and breakfast—she seemed as incongruous as a gothic church gargoyle mounted on a farmhouse.

"Returning guests," Nolan mechanically repeated. "Yes, we stayed here last year."

"You and your wife?"

"Yes."

"In that room there?"

"Yes."

"And you made arrangements to stay in the same room? You and your wife?"

Nolan nodded uncertainly—hadn't he mentioned this when he was at the front desk?

The owner's head tipped back in a slight tilt of comprehension; even at that angle the heavy lashes all but obscured her eyes, though presently an obsidian glint pierced through their thick veil. Suddenly she smiled and clapped her hands together. "That changes everything. I can't let you go now. You'll simply have to stay."

"Stay?"

"You don't want to stay?" she asked disjointedly, as if the idea of Nolan changing his mind was incomprehensible when it was he who was stunned over this unexpected reversal.

"But you said—five minutes ago you told me you were closed."

The owner merely lifted her shoulders. "I'm entitled to change my mind. Besides, it's just you and your dear little wife. I doubt the two of you will be a handful!" She cackled and gave his shoulder a playful swipe.

The odd exchange, along with the unexpected thrust of it, left Nolan in such a befuddled state that a minute later he found himself back at the front desk, where apparently he had followed the owner in order to check-in and retrieve their scant luggage.

The owner, introducing herself as Leah, presented Nolan with a document to sign, then stood watching while her guest used the capped tip of his pen to read through the dense paragraphs.

"May I see your hands, Mr. May?" she said just as Nolan finished skimming over the preliminary lines.

He looked up. "My what?"

"Your hands," Leah repeated, extending one of hers in a gesture that asked him to offer his. This evoked a childlike response in Nolan, who glanced down at his hands before placing down his pen to comply.

"Such elegant hands," Leah observed, turning them over as if they were objects of wonder. "Sinewy backs, long fingers… Are you by any chance a pianist? No? A musician then? You play some stringed instrument…"

"I don't play any instruments," said Nolan, though his plain answer did not dissuade Leah.

"What do you do then?" she pursued, eyeing his simple wedding band.

"I—teach at high school," replied Nolan, briefly distracted by the owner's stroking his palm with her thumb.

"And what do you teach?"

"Math. Can I have my hands back, please?"

For a moment, she seemed to not have heard him. Then she smiled and said, "Soft hands," before letting go.

Nolan, wishing to end the awkward exchange, picked up the pen and quickly signed the document. Leah meanwhile kept her eyes fixed on the paper, waiting for the pen's culminating flourish.

"You did well to come here, Mr. May," she said, sliding the paper away.

3

When her husband returned with their luggage, Emma rose from bed to receive her tapestry suitcase and pretended not to notice the slow smile on Nolan's face until he dropped both bags and caught her by the waist. She instinctively pushed him back, and he released her without question but kept hold of her hands.

Emma resigned to be tethered thus and stood facing him with averted eyes. She knew she was being moody, that her sudden coldness was unaccountable to him—unfair even, considering how sweet and thoughtful he was trying to be. Still, she felt justified in her stance when it was he who had been semi-absent for the past few months, coming to bed as late as possible and leaving first thing the next morning, or hiding behind a regimen of daily tasks to keep his distance, from a 5 a.m. jog followed by a shower and breakfast, to an evening of dinner, dishes and laundry, then winding down for a weekend filled with cleaning, groceries and student papers to correct. All this he did while she stayed in bed or lay on the living room couch like a husk without the mitigating lightness. And though there were times when she was grateful to have a reliable and devoted husband to handle domestic matters when she couldn't, what she wanted more than a home-cooked meal or ironed clothes was his company and with it a sense of commiseration. She wanted him to feel as dead on the inside as she was, or at least, know that he, too, was hurting in some way. Should it surprise him then that she was cold towards him now when for the past months he behaved like a saint, with all the remote benevolence of that figure?

In her peripheral vision, she saw his face hovering close to hers as he tried to slide into her line of sight. At other times, the gesture would have earned a reluctant smile from her; now, it merely brought her on the verge of tears.

"Hey," said Nolan, drawing out the word in a tender whisper. He rested his forehead on Emma's and sought her eyes, which she continued to hide behind downcast lashes. His proximity had a faint whiff of aftershave mixed with his own scent. They were miles away from their apartment, but all the same she felt a growing impulse to crawl into bed and let everything disappear.

This time Nolan did not resist when Emma withdrew her hands. The fact exasperated her: she resented his nervous aversion to emotional flare ups and inclination to disappear in a cloud of dust at the first sign; though now that they were here, she would have liked to see where he would run off to. She spared him the effort, drew a long breath and lifted her head with a steady look.

"I think I'll take a shower," she coolly announced, holding his gaze and noticing traces of a puzzled smile creeping into it. Despite herself, Emma felt her lips trembling into a smile over her husband's baffled expression and had to turn away to hide it. She thought him charming at that moment, looking dazed and on the verge of a bewildered grin—a face he made whenever he said something unintentionally funny and then wondered why she was laughing; only now he was trying to figure out whether or not there was a coy invitation in her announcing her intention to take a shower. Her stupid Nolan! Could she really stay mad at him? It would have been so easy to give in and smile, but her smile would have been like laughter wrung from anger: a reflex that sent a false signal that things were all right between them. Things were not all right between them, nor could they be resolved in one instant.

Emma went into the bathroom and closed the door behind her without sparing her husband a second glance. Inside, the space was brightly lit and replete with all manners of foliage: every shelf bore a potted plant, and every fixture was embowered in a shade of dense leaves. It was almost as if the bathroom doubled as a greenhouse, and Emma had to touch the drooping vines of a nearby ivy to verify that they were real. The room itself had not changed since their last stay, but the bathroom certainly was not like this, and she fancied herself in one of those fancy spas where the treatments were as expensive as they were sublime. Just then a shower seemed too swift an affair compared to idling here, soaking in the lush air and floating through reveries, and so Emma ran warm water into the tub, added scented oil and salts, and sat waiting for the tub to fill.

She looked about with fresh appreciation, entertaining the idea of filling their own bathroom with plants until she recalled the few unfortunate specimens that had failed to thrive under her care. The thought seemed to pull her back into a dark and familiar headspace, a place which at that instant was disagreeably incongruous with her rich surroundings. To shake it off, she checked the water level in the tub, then stood to remove her clothes, and in the process caught sight of her naked body reflected in the large mirror.

That she had a body was a fact Emma had endeavored to ignore for the past weeks, opting to change in the privacy of their small bathroom where her reflection in the square mirror stopped at the shoulders. Here, the relentless light and wall-spanning reflection revealed more stretch marks and dimpled skin than Emma cared to see. Still, she remained rooted to the spot, lifting her arm to pinch a fold of skin or smooth it back and examine the effect. Then, in a distracted haze she pulled herself away from the mirror and stepped into the tub.

The evening chill had crept into the bright bathroom, and with the tub still halfway filled the water was not enough to cover Emma, who drew her knees close and tucked one foot under the other. She was partly sensible to the cold, more occupied with the phantom of her reflection. She tried to pretend it didn't bother her: she and Nolan were nearing their tenth anniversary, and the preceding years saw them both going through seasonal shifts in weight. Nolan was apt to grow teddy-bearish around the holidays, and she would likewise indulge alongside him and gain a few pounds herself; the only difference was that often-enough Nolan's gains would melt like winter thaw, whereas she contrived and struggled to return to her regular size. And while she recalled a time when she had thick hair and a thin waistline and not the other way around, Nolan never once complained about her figure, indeed there were times when he candidly delighted in her mild weight gain, especially when it resolved into soft, buoyant curves.

No such curves graced her frame now. Emma saw with a bitter downward glance through the rising water nothing but ugly droops and sags, a cruel tally of failed pregnancies and deflated hope. Would Nolan still want her like this, she wondered? The thought intruded on her, dragging a long chain of assumptions in its wake. What if he no longer did? What if it was a sense of duty or some form of gallantry that made him keep his vows? What if he just made a show of keeping them? What if he had strayed at some point, regretted his transgression, and was moved by guilt to bring her here? God knows they had not been together for the past few months, and she knew (or rather heard) how impatient men can be…

She pictured him hurrying away from his clandestine date, clear-headed and penitent now that his needs were met. She saw him hopping into his car and stopping somewhere to change into his running gear while his clothes, bearing evidence of sin, were rumpled into a duffle bag to be furtively tossed into the washing machine. There was no evidence to back any of her assumptions, but as her friends would say, "Evidence is for the naive," or "Who needs evidence when you have intuition?"

It made little difference whether it was intuition or imagination that dictated these visions, which now erratically jumped back to the beginning of the episode. She saw Nolan park his car a block or two from the rendezvous point, taking all the necessary precautions to cover his tracks; saw him knocking on the front door of a house and be greeted by a nameless, faceless woman—what did her face matter when it was everything below it he wanted? What was it that unfaithful husbands often said in the aftermath of an affair? "Honey, I swear! She meant nothing to me. It was just an itch to scratch."

Emma began pounding her leg with a fist in a slow, mechanical rhythm. "Useless bag of flesh," she thought, feeling betrayed by her body and resorting to mental flogs since the physical ones hurt less. On she went, hurling insult and goading tears until her blank expression began to crumple.

She wept in silence at first, though soon her sobs grew hitched, and the small sharp sound drew Nolan's attention.

"Honey?" she heard him calling through the door. The concern in his voice sickened her. She wanted to be left alone to cry and wail and be torn by all the rampant emotions boiling inside her.

"Honey?" Nolan called again and began to open the door.

Emma emerged dripping from the bathtub, and with a wrenched cry slammed the door shut.

4

The lobby was dark save for the table lamps casting pale circles of orange light, and between them Nolan sank in one of the sofas and leaned his head back, removing his glasses to rub the bridge of his nose.

It was warm here, the stillness and emptiness deepening his sense of isolation, as if the seating area was encased in a bell jar. The effect would have been complete had Nolan not been attuned to the room upstairs, listening for any muffled sound Emma might make. Back home, he would be spending the hour preparing dinner for the two of them, and even without the TV going in the living room, the city noise outside or incidental racket of the other tenants would bleed through to fill the dreadful quiet. Here, in the absence of other guests, Nolan had the awkward sense of intruding on some stranger's home instead of staying at a bed and breakfast. Never before, not even in the past months had it sunk in how lonely he felt without Emma. She was the center of his world, and her company alone would make even a tundra wasteland feel less stark and dreary. It all seemed so straightforward bringing her here to lift her spirits, yet even his best efforts brought him nothing but anger and resentment. What should he do? What did she want him to do?

Nolan sat facing the unlit fireplace, which in their past stay had always been kindled and tended to by the owners. Perhaps it was foolish of him to have come here expecting a repeat of last year. The place had changed and not even the original owners were around to welcome them back. He began to speculate on the lot of the previous owners, whether they had sold the business to retire, or whether one or both of them had passed on and the place was left to an inexperienced relative who found herself overwhelmed and at a dire moment decided to downsize and let the staff go. The latter, at least, explained the odd reception as well as the owner's sudden change of mind, deciding to let them stay on a whim. Whatever the case was, she certainly wasted little time making the place hers…

Nolan's eyes crept up the mantle towards the thicket of potted plants and drifted over the surrounding walls where one of the masks fixed his attention. He had yet to restore his glasses, and through the dim haze the mask's shadowy features waxed murky and unsettling. The combination of silence and graven images never sat well with Nolan, and even without glasses, he could never stare long at an inanimate face without sensing some unseen presence.

It's like being in a room full of trophy heads, he thought, trying to define the sensation but finding the analogy lacking. Despite his unease, Nolan felt no strong incentive to return to his room, and so laid his head back and tried to forget the grimacing faces.

"Mr. May?"

The voice gave Nolan a start. He opened his eyes and discovered the blurred outline of the owner standing at his side.

"Is everything all right, Mr. May?"

"Yes," he answered, sliding his glasses back on, and wondering if he had fallen asleep to not have heard her approaching. "Everything's fine. I just came down here for…" he trailed off, unable to find a good excuse for sitting alone in the dark.

"For dinner?" suggested the owner.

He looked up at her. "Dinner?"

"It's included in your reservation."

Nolan recalled no such arrangement and was about to say something to that effect when she added, motioning towards the corridor that led up to the dining room. "It's a complimentary meal—no extra charge. I've already set it up for you."

Though the dining room and its neighboring kitchen were little more than twenty steps from the lobby, no smell of cooking filled the air—at least none Nolan could discern over the owner's ever-present air of acrid smoke. Still, hours had passed since Nolan last ate, and even the prospect of reheated soup or cold sandwiches was enough to make him rise out of his seat and take a few steps before remembering Emma.

"I'll go and call your wife," said the owner, already ascending the stairs. "You just go right ahead."

Nolan obeyed, somewhat relieved to have her go in his stead. She had a better chance at persuading Emma, who even in her bitterest moods was not likely to decline their host's invitation. He heard the soft knocks upstairs, yawned and stretched his arms overhead, then headed to the dining room. There he found the ten-seater walnut table and took his seat near the head, where presumably the owner sat. Sure enough, she came in and took her designated seat.

"Where's Emma?" Nolan asked when his wife didn't follow.

The owner, uncovering the main dish, plainly said, "She said she didn't want any dinner." Without looking up she laid an arresting hand on Nolan's arm to keep him from getting up.

"She'll be all right, Mr. May, she just needs some time alone. Please, sit down."

Nolan, who was still in the process of rising from his chair, remained hovering over his seat a few seconds longer before he figured he probably would not have better luck if he went upstairs himself. He yielded reluctantly to the pressure on his arm and sat down, staring across the table at the empty seat, still gnawed by guilt and a sense of duty. In the meantime the owner had taken his plate and filled it with sliced steak and potatoes covered in mushroom gravy.

"You'd do well to keep some distance," she said, gesturing with the serving fork before piercing a slice of beef and carrying it to her plate. "All that care and attention," she added, sounding almost derisive, "does nothing but smother her. No wonder she lashed out like that. I know I would."

For a moment, Nolan remained transfixed by the sight of his heaped-up plate, allowing time for the owner's words to sink in. When they did, he tried to meet her eyes and ask her how she knew, but on reflection he surmised she must have heard the bathroom door slam shut, then found him in the lobby and put two and two together.

"You're right," he conceded, more to put the matter to rest than out of conviction. The last thing he needed was meddling from a stranger, however good her intentions were. "Thank you for the meal," he said, picking up his fork and knife.

"Sorry you had to go through all that trouble for us."

"Oh, it's nothing," she said, smiling over the bit of meat she was sawing with her knife. "I only hope it's to your liking. I like mine juicy and rare, but I thought it was safer to go with well-done. Try it with the sauce, it's absolutely divine! I'm only sorry your wife won't get a taste of it. I'll set aside a plate for her in case she changes her mind. How long have you two been married?"

Nolan pretended to focus on his meal to avoid her inquiring gaze. He did not like the prying curiosity behind her question and tried to stall, pretending to chew a tough morsel, hoping she would lose interest and move on to a different topic. Her gaze persisted, and so he gave in. "About ten years."

Her thick black lashes cast a heavy shadow over her eyes, yet through them Nolan caught a twinkle of victory as she smiled. "And how long have you two known each other?"

"We go a while back," he said, seeking refuge in a nebulous answer. But if anything the ambiguity stoked her interest.

"Ten years—and you're a high school teacher—and you can't be older than forty, or at least you don't look it. That must mean… you met in college, right?"

It was tempting to give a false answer just then, just to throw her off. But he somehow suspected his wife would be subjected to the same probing and it would not look good on his part to fudge the details. Nolan straightened his back. "High school, actually. Only we waited till after college to get married. What about you?" he hastily added before she had a chance to barge in with another question. "Is there someone in your life? I never got your last name."

"Oh!" she waved him off with a chuckle. "It's fine. Just call me Leah."

"Well, then, Leah," Nolan raised a forkful of beef, "my compliments to the chef."

"Have you tried the mushrooms? They're morels, you know."

"Are they? I don't think I've ever had them before…"

With that, the topic turned to foraging and preparing wild mushrooms, and Nolan congratulated himself on successfully diverting the conversation away from private affairs. He had a sense she was a question or two shy of asking why they were here—no, really: why did they come here?—and what would he tell her then? That they've been having trouble conceiving? That after two miscarriages the third seemed promising? That they were not counting but secretly counting each week, so that when they reached the thirty-sixth and she began to have pain they thought they still had a chance? And when their daughter had died before she was born he felt nothing? That after that, Emma seemed indifferent to both his presence and his absence, and so he left her each morning with a tender kiss before heading out, mortified to discover the atmosphere outside was far less stifling. Would he number the weeks that merged into months, during which he took more work, took longer routes driving home, and soon took up running to fill in that last gap of free time? Night after night, he prepared dinner or brought home takeout and coaxed Emma to eat something. It became part of their routine for her to precede him into the bedroom while he washed dishes, wiped the counters, and loaded the washing machine, and after he had turned off the lights and crept into bed, he could tell from her silence that she was not asleep, but lay curled up, her body tighter than a knot, refusing to let go of the loss. He dearly—hopelessly loved his wife, but he felt helpless in the face of the grief that had settled over their marriage like volcanic ash.

That's why we're here, concluded Nolan's inner voice, ever more eloquent than his tongue. *We're here because I want to go back to where we were last year—before the pregnancy and the false hopes. I want to erase them. I want a do-over—I want to rewind that tape and record over it and forget the past eleven months had ever happened.*

Thus ran the answer in Nolan's head without uttering a single word, and while he listened to his own thoughts, his body went through the motions of eating and nodding in response to Leah's ramblings. She stopped suddenly, and it took him a second or two to notice the abrupt quiet until he looked up and found her staring at him. The silence stretched on, her inscrutable eyes fixed on him. Then, without warning, she extended a finger towards his face, traced a line down his cheek near the mouth. So surprised he was by the gesture that he froze, not knowing what she was doing or how to react until she pulled her hand back and presented a reddish brown smear of something she had wiped off his face.

"You had a bit of sauce," she explained, putting the tip of her finger to her lips.

When Nolan returned to their room, he found Emma wrapped in a bathrobe and laying on the bedcover in her usual curled up position. The lights were on, and she lay with her back to him, but his unease melted into tender sadness as soon as he noted an air of peace in her soft breathing and found courage to edge to the other side to make sure she slept. He stood appreciating the sight for a few moments before fetching an extra blanket from the closet to cover her.

As he spread the blanket over his sleeping wife, the bed skirt brushed over his foot, and he remembered the infant doll he had kicked under the bed. In all likelihood, the silly thing would remain undiscovered until after their departure, yet knowing it was there with the slim chance of Emma finding it while reaching for bedroom slippers was compelling enough for Nolan to kneel down and stick his arm under the bed. After a few unsuccessful sweeps, he lay on his stomach to push his arm further in, then tried the same with the other side of the bed, grumbling, groping, and growing all the more stubborn because he knew the damned thing was there if only his finger would brush against it.

Finally he stood up and dusted himself off, convinced he needed a flashlight to find it, or would have more luck in the morning, when sunlight filled the room.

5

At some dark hour of night, Nolan was roused from sleep by the sensation of someone clinging to him.

He did not recall sitting up, or the transition that led from him lying on his side of the bed to being caught up and held tight. Indeed, he had to touch the head buried against his chest and feel the soft curls to realize it was Emma who now clung to him in a frightened, desperate way: One of her arms was wrapped around his neck, the other was thrown over his shoulder, and both hands clutched fistfuls of his t-shirt's fabric. Her face felt hot, and the sharp, hitched sound that came from her was closer to sobbing, though without looking at her face it was impossible to tell whether she laughed or wept.

"Emma," he said, his tongue still heavy with sleep even as his heart hammered.

The long, thin whine she gave spiked to a sharp cry when he tried to reach for his glasses. She held him fast, as though they stood on the edge of a cliff and he was the only thing that kept her from falling.

"It's okay—it's okay," he said, rubbing her back. One of her hands let go, and he fancied she extended her arm, perhaps pointing at something behind him. He strained to look over his shoulder, but being in a constrained position as well as doubly blinded by the thick dark and nearsightedness, Nolan failed to see anything at all. Again, he tried to reach for his glasses or the table lamp switch only for Emma to seize him with renewed fervor, and for the sake of his sanity, Nolan had to convince himself that nothing stood there—that Emma was experiencing some sort of night terror. And yet it seemed unbearable at that moment to have Leah barging in to check on them. His mind was on high alert, turning on him with the arbitrary suggestion that it was Leah who stood unseen in that dark corner, and the notion deeply unsettled Nolan while he went on hushing his wife and mechanically stroking her back.

Whether from spent energy or returning sleep, her hands soon relaxed, allowing Nolan to lean back and make a clumsy grab at his glasses. He slipped them on only to realize how little they helped without light. But having managed as much, he was able to rearrange himself into a partial recline while still holding the body slumped against him until he lay half-supine with his wife's head on his chest. From that position he was free to turn his head and look in the direction she had been pointing at, if just to reassure himself that nothing was there. By then his eyesight had adjusted, and even in the enveloping dark he began to detect a tall and narrow shade in the corner of the room.

Nolan kept his eyes fixed on it while he reached for the table lamp on his nightstand. The longer he stared, the less he was able to understand what it was. At first it appeared to have no corporeal dimensions—more like a black stain issuing from the wall, yet, unlike a stain, it was not static but wavered in an irregular motion akin to that of long drapes stirred by air. All this Nolan attributed to tricks of vision—that is, until he heard the rustle of fabric, and his reeling mind froze and fell silent.

His groping hand found the lamp's light switch, yet Nolan trembled between remaining in the dark and discovering what it was that stood there. The answer came when he flipped the switch and the towering shadow in the corner disappeared in the first flash of light.

6

Emma looked up from her plate of scrambled eggs and studied Nolan who sat listlessly across the table from her. Signs of troubled sleep told on him: he had his elbows on the table and was using them to keep his head propped on his fists. Behind his glasses his eyes, weighed down by heavy lids, tried to focus on her while he repeated a question she had evidently missed.

"I said how'd you sleep last night?"

Emma, suspending a forkful of scrambled eggs halfway to her mouth, paused to consider the question. "Okay, I guess. Why?" she said before the fork resumed its course.

"You woke up in the middle of the night. You sounded scared—you were crying."

"Was I?" She frowned. "Funny—I don't remember dreaming or anything. All I remember is lying in bed and that's it."

Nolan nodded, more interested in returning to his coffee than pursuing the matter. His diverted attention allowed Emma to enjoy the sight of her husband, who closed his eyes as if succumbing to sleep even as he lifted the coffee cup to his lips, gave a faint sip, then went back to resting his head on one hand. Culminating this study of sleep deprivation was the disheveled blond hair, the sandy tufts of which brushed over the handles of his glasses. Emma smiled to herself, thinking how adorable her husband looked. Like his unshaven cheek, his voice had that morning rasp that gave it a salty edge. He had the sober, low voice of a mid-century reporter and a warm, gentle delivery that would have made him a star narrator were it not for his natural shyness. His voice carried well-enough within the confines of a classroom, but placed in front of a microphone, even to read from a script, Nolan was apt to mumble, grow red-faced and giggle—something they had discovered not too long ago when he was looking for ways to supplement his income and tried auditioning for a voice-over job. Back then, she was six months pregnant and the two of them had made tentative plans to furnish a nursery…

Emma's knife, which had been cutting into a sausage, slowed to a stop. She stared down at her half-eaten breakfast with a growing sense of inner wonder. Her mind had inadvertently drifted towards a subject which never failed to afflict her with penetrating sorrow, only now she found herself skirting its peripheries without ill-effect. The core matter—the loss itself and the episode surrounding it—still radiated a foreboding grief that kept her from approaching. It was like staring from afar at a crater with crumbling edges, knowing it would not close up anytime soon if ever, yet without feeling like it would swallow her either. It was true that she had suffered past losses and eventually recovered from them, but the last was more promising, seemed likeliest to come through, and was therefore the hardest-hitting of all three. If, in the past, she had rallied in a matter of weeks, her latter grief stretched on for months without any perceptible decline. No doubt the crater was still there, but the dust had settled, and the surrounding air had grown clear. Was it really this trip that instigated this—a simple change of scenery—or did last night's sleep wash away the emotional deadwood that had amassed in her?

Emma looked about the breakfast table shining in the morning light, surveyed the sun-gilt china and silverware, then closed her eyes and drew a long breath, as if pressing a bouquet of flowers to her face. There was magic in this place—not the stuff of fairytales, but a likewise intangible quality. Would that she could press these moments between the pages of a book… She felt light—much lighter than she had felt in ages. This morning she found the energy to get out of bed, brush her teeth, tie her hair up in a loose bun, and was happy to see her favorite wool skirt and sweater were among the items Nolan had packed for her.

The man in question had dosed off, jaw slack and mouth slightly open, his head still propped on one hand. Emma broke off a morsel of toast and tossed it at him, then broke off another and leaned forward for better range. Two more morsels missed the target and pelted his face. He slowly opened his eyes, found his wife laughing and smiled himself.

"The weather looks good," he said after he had finished his coffee. "We should go for a walk in the woods."

She shook her head, wrinkling her nose at the suggestion. "Let's not do that."

"Why not? It'll do you good."

The answer made her pause and put down her fork and knife. "Do me good… how?"

"Well, the fresh air and exercise will be good for you."

"Some other time. I'd really rather we stay in," she quietly insisted, hoping her husband would get the hint.

"But you love hiking in the woods here. Remember last year? We walked and walked until we found that circular clearing surrounded by trees. Remember that spot?"

Emma did remember the spot, the shaded walk up to it, the picnic basket they had carried, the blanket they spread, the clement sky above and the crunch of leaves underneath as Nolan laid her down and began to kiss her. But that was then. Judging by the past few weeks, this outing promised to be a chaste affair. He seemed keen on repeating everything they had done last year, as if storing up quality time against a season of neglect. It harkened back to Emma's father making up for long spells of absence through gifts and impromptu day trips, through boisterous displays of affection that lasted a few hours and a string of promises that were sooner broken than kept. Only now it was her husband whose pleading eyes searched her face for hints of a reluctant acquiescence, and she was saved from having to commit herself one way or another by Leah swooping down on them.

"Good morning!" she sang, placing her hands on Emma's chair. "How are you, my dear? I didn't make your proper acquaintance last night. I'm the owner here, but you can call me Leah." She gave Emma's hand a quick shake before leaning back, as if awestruck. "Why, Mr. May! You didn't tell me what a curly-haired angel your wife is. Look at those soulful eyes—she's practically a baby!" added Leah with an ostentatious nudge. "Are you sure she's your wife and not one of your students? Look at that fresh face. I could take a bite out of it!" She cackled and sidled up to Nolan with clasped hands. "How's breakfast? I hope the food's to your liking."

Nolan, dabbing his mouth with a napkin, hurried to say, "Everything's great."

"Wonderful! And what do you plan on doing today?" she inquired, draping her hand on the back of Nolan's chair.

He glanced at the long fingers brushing his shoulder and seemed about to inch away but covered his inclination with an answer. "Well, we were thinking of going for a walk—"

The owner cut him off with a cry. "A walk! Doesn't that sound lovely? I was thinking of doing that myself. Perhaps I'll join you."

Emma gave her husband a look of protest. "Nolan—"

"We were thinking of going off on our own," her husband promptly explained.

Leah nodded. "You're right, of course. Well at least let me make you a hamper basket. Why settle for just a walk when you can have a picnic?"

The kind offer surprised Nolan into stammering a word of thanks, while Emma, conscious of Leah's presence, whispered across the table, "Nolan, I told you I don't want to go."

Nolan turned to his angel with gentle concern. "Honey, the trail's beautiful this time of day, and we're only here on a short stay. Come on, a ten minute stroll just to get some fresh air. It'll do you a world of good, I promise."

His hands, resting on the table, made a small tentative reach for hers, and while the look in his eyes touched Emma, she kept her hands folded in her lap. Already she felt a stealing inclination to return to bed, and wanted to tell him as much, hinting that they can still enjoy their stay here without having to leave their room—surely the possibility had crossed his mind—after all, they did more than take leisurely walks into the woods during their previous stay. But with her husband being dense and the owner standing close, it was hard to convey this, short of spelling it out straight. "Why do you always insist on doing what you want to do?" she finally brought out in frustration, and was doubly hurt by the pained look on her husband's face, as if she had slapped an offering out of his hand.

Emma was about to leave the table when Leah came to her side and laid a hand on her shoulder. "You don't have to go if you don't want to. You're more than welcome to stay here all day and put your feet up, if you like."

The meddlesome remark, softened by the note of hospitality, drew a gracious smile from Emma, who turned to thank her hostess. Nolan was less touched by the gesture, and the intent way he stared at Leah made Emma a trifle uneasy. She knew her husband didn't have a mean bone in his body, and would rarely if ever utter an unkind word to anyone, but this fact made his reticent anger all the more potent whenever she chanced to sense it brewing under that quiet exterior.

7

"Are you sure you don't want to go?"

Emma lowered the book she was reading to regard her husband. Apparently the fact that she had settled in the lobby with a book borrowed from the guest's library did not deter him from pressing his case. Wearing her down with repeated requests was his gentle art of persuasion, surpassed only by repeated kisses whenever he was trying to have his way with her. The latter currency would have more likely purchased her compliance, but Nolan was nothing if not single-minded, and it would have never crossed his mind to switch tactics. Yet so seldom did he nag her into anything, it showed how much he wanted her to go on that stupid walk with him.

"I told you I'd very much rather stay in," she answered in a quiet tone meant to discourage him from pushing the matter.

"But it's such a nice day." Nolan indicated the window through which clear skies filled the room with powder blue light.

"Well, we can still enjoy it here," Emma rejoined, propping her ankles on the footrest. She had one of the windows opened a crack, and the lingering morning chill had suffused the house with a crisp air so delicious that she decided to forgo lying in bed in favor of lounging here with a book; her husband's quiet company would have completed this delightful picture, especially if a shared blanket or a flickering fire on the hearth were involved. To her chagrin, Nolan gave up on asking her to join him and went out himself, saying he would be back in an hour or so.

After he left, Emma smiled briefly to herself, remembering how her husband—bundled to his beaky nose in a blue anorak and scarf—had solemnly reassured her he'll be back, as though embarking on some dangerous mission. Her gallant Nolan!—imagining she would fall apart in his absence. In spite of their disagreement, her light mood prevailed even to the point of finding his fretful behavior almost touching, though it would have been far more touching if he had chosen to stay with her.

Minutes passed, and the book Emma had held up to read slowly dipped below her line of vision until it lay open in her lap. She felt a prick of remorse, not from refusing to follow her husband's plan, but over a missed opportunity. It was an echo of childhood, when her family would go out for ice-cream, and she—out of spite for her mother who was unfair to her over some matter, or a sister who had insulted her—would refuse to come along until the offending party apologized and earned her forgiveness. So she was left behind, and from the living room window she would watch the family car drive off without her, waiting in vain for it to turn around. Her tactics never came to fruition, yet she never quite cured herself of the method. And now here she was, well into adulthood and still relying on the same strategy of holding her ground whenever she perceived herself the injured party in some way. They came here to spend the weekend together, and still Nolan carried on in the same way he did back home.

A phantom of last night's mood washed over Emma with all its strident thoughts, and she stared at what could only be deemed as a warning sign that their marriage was in trouble. All at once the airy room felt close and oppressive. She set the book down and rose, suddenly craving a glass of water.

After trying the front desk and dining room for the owner, Emma followed the tiled floor into the kitchen, the door of which was left wide open, letting out a pungent breath of cooking and concealing the "Staff Only" sign. The kitchen itself was less of a utilitarian space and more a humid little bower filled with potted plants and overhung with bundles of herbs strung from wooden beams; instead of appliances, the countertops were lined with opaque jars; instead of decorative tableware, the recessed shelves were teeming with pink stuff that, from a distance, seemed like clusters of rose leaves.

Emma forgot about the glass of water and went in for a closer look, drawn by the vibrant color against a dull background, and discovering on approach that what she took for flower petals were in fact the gilled undersides of pink mushrooms pushing their thin caps upwards. There were rows and layers of them growing out of the recessed shelves, so much so that their abundance covered the medium from which they spawned. For a moment or two, Emma stood admiring the robust specimens, her lifted finger poised to touch the delicate folds. She turned to survey the rest of the kitchen, and her gaze landed on a table a few feet away where she caught sight of what appeared to be a raw chicken laid out on a wooden board. It was the briefest of glimpses, for no sooner did it register when a pair of hands clamped over her eyes.

"Who allowed you in my kitchen?"

Emma froze on the spot, recognizing the owner yet unable to shake off the initial shock which momentarily robbed her of her own voice. The sensation was made more stifling by the hands covering her eyes, and the sweet, pungent odor that reminded Emma of goats.

"I'm so sorry," she stammered, making a feeble attempt to detach herself, "I didn't mean to—I just wanted a glass of water, and I looked for you in the lobby and dining room—"

While she fumbled for words, Emma felt the hands turn her head and firmly guide her out of the kitchen and into the lobby. Once there, the owner removed her hands and stood facing her guest who despite being shaken by the incident was far more mortified by her apparent transgression.

"I'm so sorry," she reiterated, her apology sounding inadequate to her ears.

The owner tilted her gaunt head back with a stern look, eyes peering through frightfully thick lashes. Then suddenly her features relaxed into a benign expression as she reached out and touched Emma's head in an affectionate pat that ended with her fingering a few strands of hair.

"Poor lamb," she said in a velvety voice. "Was it thirsty and wanted something to drink?"

Emma shrank from her touch but stood in place with her hands down like a penitent student. Indeed, she felt herself in the presence of one of those teachers with a capricious temperament who often had an awkward way of painting their face that made them look older than they were. In an empathetic flash Emma saw how such a face would draw grimaces behind the lady's back—the kind of covert looks she and her fellow students used to pass each other whenever a teacher of colorful appearance entered the classroom or passed them in the hall—and the perception made Emma feel almost sorry for her, more so since she herself was apt to share a furtive laugh or two at the teacher's expense.

"Is your husband around?"

"He went out for a walk."

Leah smiled. "It's just the two of us then."

The following minutes saw the two ladies seated in a room upstairs, which Emma surmised was the owner's private room or study—or what she pictured the word 'boudoir' implied whenever she came across it in a nineteenth-century novel. The rich interior alone invited a prolonged study had not an instinct of shyness kept Emma from looking about lest she comes across as nosy and prying—something she was all too conscious of just then; instead, she fixed her attention on the tea tray the owner had set on the round table between them, and the long, translucent arc of liquid Leah made pouring tea into eggshell cups.

"I hope you don't mind having tea here instead of the lobby," she said, handing Emma a filled cup. "I usually have it here and thought it easier to invite you over."

"Oh, but it's such a nice room," Emma broke out, happy to have hit on an excuse to look about and glance over the shelves and table tops brimming with flowering plants. Her tentative observation carried over to a wall where a length of braided rope was mounted lengthwise over an old tapestry, the lower half of which cascaded behind a glass cabinet and made a splendid background for primitive clay figures.

"Good," said Leah. "I'm glad we could sit and talk in private—just us girls." She beamed on her guest, who promptly returned the smile. "I didn't want to risk your husband walking in or overhearing us," she began, and a look of bewilderment must have manifested on Emma's face for Leah to follow up with, "Oh, it's nothing, lamb. I just wanted to ask if everything is all right between you and your husband."

The clarification did little to chase away the clouded look on Emma's face. In the past she met such queries with a gentle scoff and a smiling reassurance that things were more than all right, but now, her instinctive bright response faltered under fresh doubts as she began to wonder whether Leah had noticed something untoward about Nolan, perhaps catching him making a furtive phone call last night and overhearing an intimate exchange between him and the person on the other end. The notion passed in a flash, and to her credit, Emma tried to curb her imagination, though she could neither deny nor explain Nolan's prolonged absence the previous evening.

"Why wouldn't things be all right between me and Nolan?" she said at length.

Leah, who was stirring sugar into her tea, looked up from her task but not directly at Emma. "Well I don't mean to pry," she said through a small, self-deprecating chuckle, "but when it comes to certain matters—when a person's safety is in question…"

"Safety?"

"I heard you crying last night."

"Oh," murmured Emma, remembering what Nolan had said over breakfast. "I guess I was having a bad dream—"

Leah spoke over her. "Did your husband hurt you in any way?"

Emma's face colored as she uttered a nervous laugh. "Who? Nolan?" Her unaccountable nervousness bubbled over into another laugh. "I don't think he's capable of hurting anyone, let alone me!"

Again, Leah tilted her head to stare down her nose. She appeared skeptical, as if Emma was fibbing to protect her husband; her disapproving silence was bad enough, but it was the way she angled her head to affect a reproachful stare that bothered Emma, as if the owner was peering through the eye slits of a mask. Finally, she gave up on trying to stare the truth out of her guest, smoothing her pressed lips to return to her tea.

"Are you having trouble sleeping, lamb?"

The question surprised Emma almost as much as the pet name. "Not really. Most nights I sleep soundly."

"Like a baby?"

Emma fiddled with her tea cup before nodding. "You could say that."

"Except for last night."

"I don't know about last night. Nolan said the same thing, that I was crying. But I don't remember anything at all. I suppose it's for the best, though. Maybe it's something subconscious, you know? Maybe it's the past few months…" she trailed off, lifting her cup to take a sip of tea. The warm liquid helped her dry throat, and in that brief reprieve she was able to steady her voice. She cleared her throat and resumed, assuming an air of detachment at odds with her roving gaze. "Maybe it's just old memories—Did Nolan ever tell you we spent a weekend here last year? We had such a lovely time. It was the typical quiet getaway you dream of taking, away from everything. No work, no friends or family to drop in and interrupt your time together. It was just us in this beautiful little slice of heaven. We were so happy… and we didn't know it at the time, but we were—I was—"

She stopped for another sip, trying to down the lump in her throat. Her bright mood that morning had cheated her into believing her past was well behind her, and that she could finally broach the painful subject. Vestiges of ill-timed laughter still rattled inside her. Why had the conversation taken this turn? And yet she found herself desperate to talk about it and release this caged-up thing in a way she never could with her husband because he was bound to freeze or fly at the subject; however, she was equally mortified at the thought of unburdening herself in front of a stranger, however kind she seemed to be.

Emma kept her eyes on the cup she held on her knees, blinking back tears, wishing she had a napkin or some tissues to dab her nose. To speak or even budge would crack her blank expression—she may as well have endeavored to balance a brimming jug on her head without spilling a drop. So focused was she on her hands and the cup and saucer they encircled that Emma failed to notice any movement until Leah placed her hands over Emma's. The compassionate touch was enough to loosen Emma's locked anguish and she bowed her head in a futile attempt at hiding a grimace that furrowed her features. Her contained sobs were deep and hideously ragged, reverberating through the close embrace Leah offered. After the worst of it had passed, Emma lifted her head off her hostess's shoulder with an embarrassment that deepened the color of her heated face. She tried to curb her weeping, and was only successful after she saw Leah looking at her with a face transformed—the corners of her thin mouth dragged down while the inner tips of her brows puckered up, presenting a maudlin reflection of Emma's pained countenance, almost to the point of mockery.

Soon the look melted away, and she placed her hands on either side of Emma's head, bent it down and kissed her forehead.

"Why don't you tell me all about it, lamb?" she said, modulating her voice to a low and velvety pitch.

Emma stared back with red-rimmed eyes, startled first by the unexpected gesture, then by the residual cold those lips left on her forehead.

8

In spite of his original plan to spend time with his wife, Nolan needed the solitary walk to clear his head and alleviate his mounting frustration. Over breakfast things seemed to have taken a turn for the better, and Emma's bright laugh shone on him like sunlight after a long and dreary winter. Then, like an idiot, he went and soured the mood by insisting they go out for a walk, never stopping to consider whether Emma might be tired or lacking energy after a long period of inactivity, so that even a stroll felt like a demanding task. Exercise was not the point—Nolan himself did not think to pack his running shoes for the weekend—all he wanted was to have Emma alone to himself, away from the meddlesome owner and her constant hovering.

He trudged on, putting one foot in front of the other, all the while kicking himself for not suggesting they go for a leisurely drive instead. It did not escape him that Emma preferred they went back upstairs and stayed there for the remainder of the day, yet he had the sense that even in the privacy of their room the two of them would somehow be observed like rabbits in a cage. Perhaps he was exaggerating, yet the feeling was hard to shake off, more so after last night's disturbing episode, the way his wife pointed to that corner and the indelible sense that someone was indeed there. The remembrance of that night alone was enough to stir echoes of Emma's terrified cries. To drown it out, Nolan turned his hearing outwards to focus on the distant chirps resounding through the emptiness alongside the moist crunch of brown leaves underfoot. Soon he came upon the clearing where they had picnicked last year, and the sight of it made Nolan yearn for his wife. The spot was unchanged, and even in this open space Nolan fancied he and Emma could enjoy an intimate hour or two, sheltered among the trees, far from prying ears and eyes. Such visions were enough to send him rushing back to Emma's side, yet he remained rooted to the spot, confronting the source of his cold feet.

After all, how soon was too soon?

Surely enough time had passed, but a part of him—the part that still carried the weight of weeks past—still balked at the idea of trying, or rather he did not want to try for another, ever.

The subject of birth control had long been left in his wife's hands. They were both comfortable with the arrangement, and before embarking on this trip he made sure to pack her pill case, understanding that she should continue to take them like clockwork. Everything should be fine as long as they were careful in that regard and given that they had trouble conceiving in the past, Nolan estimated the odds were in their favor.

It occurred to him then that at some point last year Emma must have decided to stop taking her pills in order for her to conceive. He did not recall discussing the matter with her, nor could he pinpoint when she had made the decision—whether she had decided herself, or whether the pregnancy was the result of a one-time lapse; all he recalled was that winter morning, the heavy snowfalls outside their apartment window, and him standing in front of the TV, coffee in hand, waiting for the inevitable Snow Day announcement; Emma had emerged from the bathroom, eyes shining with happy tears, holding something that from a distance resembled a white thermometer, and which made Nolan's stomach drop as soon as he recognized it. Her third pregnancy and yet she still had beamed with a touch of triumph, perhaps surprised she managed to beat the odds. It had taken Nolan a few seconds to muster a smile for her sake, and he was thankful that in the interval any hint of dread in his eyes was well-concealed behind a vacant stare.

Several months later, after the worst had come to pass, Emma refused to leave the house for a follow up appointment with the obstetrician, leaving Nolan to see the specialist in her stead. In a way, Nolan was glad to have a one-on-one consultation, taking the opportunity to inquire if there was anything wrong with him—if the loss was somehow his fault.

The good doctor took a minute to skim through their file before answering with impersonal sympathy. "Nothing wrong with you," and flipping through his wife's profile, he added, "Nothing wrong with her either. Thirty-three is relatively young, but—age could be a factor. Genetics, too, in some cases. Some couples have trouble conceiving with each other, but they go on popping babies like bunnies with other partners."

That last part haunted Nolan, and he was thankful Emma was not there to hear it. That they remained childless meant nothing to him as long as they had each other. The question was whether she shared his sentiments, or whether the prospect of a childless marriage would be reason enough for her to leave him. There were alternatives, of course. The topic of adoption had come up some time after the second miscarriage and before their last attempt; it was first suggested by well-meaning friends, and then brought up again in private, but the timing proved ill and Emma was too bitter to even consider it as an option.

Nolan turned away from the forest clearing and began making his way back to the bed and breakfast, anxious to return to his wife. Caution be damned! If he could make her happy this weekend, if he could isolate the two of them in an enchanted pocket of time…

Less than an hour later, he stood at the front door, scraping the bottom of his sneakers on the welcome mat before entering. "Em?" he called, his voice echoing in the empty lobby. He climbed the stairs to check his room and there found a note left for him on the antique birch vanity.

Gone out with Leah, it read. *Back by dinner*.

Nolan read the note again, uncertain whether to feel glad that she had finally agreed to leave the house, or apprehensive that she was out with Leah. Then he felt somewhat ashamed for judging the owner who so far had been kind and accommodating. No one was free from flaws, but if Leah was eccentric and intrusive, she was also thoughtful and apparently sagacious if she managed to coax Emma to join her on presumably some daily errand. In the meantime, he had the entire house to himself and at least half a day to pass before dinner.

He lay in bed, intending to rest for a minute or two, and woke up to discover he had slept through lunch and into well-past three in the afternoon, and he wandered out into the hallway and called for his wife, hoping the dinner she mentioned in her note indicated an early supper. No answer, but while he stood in the hallway, Nolan caught a sound pecking through the quiet. Faint as it was, the corridor being narrow and compact made it easy to place the source, beckoning Nolan to the other end of the hall until he reached a closed door.

The door stood solitary in the shadowy section of the upper floor, untouched by the afternoon light slanting through the hallway windows, and through the paneled wood came the staccato taps that led him here. It sounded low, on the same level as his ankles, leading Nolan to believe an animal was on the other side—perhaps a pet Leah kept shut up in her room so as not to disturb the guests. As he turned to leave, the taps became louder, as if the creature on the other side had somehow sensed Nolan moving away. It was enough to make him pause before finally leaving, reminding himself that he was a guest in this house and that it was no business of his what she kept or did behind closed doors.

By the time Emma returned, she found Nolan in the backyard chopping wood for the fireplace. She ran up to him, tilting her basket with a giddy smile to show him the medley of mushrooms she and Leah had been gathering all day.

Nolan, growing a little heated from his task, was glad for a chance to put down the axe and peer into the lifted basket. He conceded with raised eyebrows that their number and variety were indeed remarkable, saying, "You picked all these by yourselves? You didn't raid some farmers' market and make out like bandits?" He was on the verge of asking how long it took them to gather this small heap if they were gone all morning and a good deal of the afternoon, but his previous comment was met with a lighthearted laugh, and his angel's radiant, pink cheeks were enough to make him swallow his tongue.

"I'm going to prepare them for dinner," she said, hurrying back into the house, and it was then that Nolan noticed she only had one shoe on.

While Emma was allowed into the kitchen to help with dinner preparations, Nolan was barred from entering and made to observe the "Staff Only" sign on the door. Through his wife, however, he managed to gain permission to light a fire in the lobby. Despite his general sober disposition, Nolan found himself smiling with almost boyish excitement (perhaps infected by Emma's high spirits) as he knelt down to arrange the pieces of wood.

When he was satisfied with the arrangement, he began looking about for a box of matches, and in the wide sweep of his survey his eyes fell on the armchair he had sat in the previous evening. There, tucked between the arm and cushion seat was the infant doll, bald and pucker-mouthed, reaching to him with outstretched hands.

An unpleasant shock bristled through Nolan when for a brief moment he fancied he had found the same doll from his bedroom. Then doubt set in as he noted a few differences—the bedroom doll was a more realistic model with moving eyelids, whereas this had exaggerated oval eyes that were painted on. Nolan confirmed this himself when he picked up the naked doll and flung it out of the front door.

Dinner was a veritable forager's feast featuring creamy soup, a herb salad, and sautéed mushrooms sprinkled with cracked pepper that left a lingering warmth on the tongue.

"Your wife was so helpful this meal almost pays for itself," Leah joked, though Nolan expected the meal to show up on his bill. Still, Emma's smile at the compliment made it all worthwhile; how gladly Nolan would have paid his heart's blood to have her always smiling like this.

9

She smelled sweet like maple syrup that evening, and after they had gone up to their room and fell into bed, Nolan fancied he could taste it on her skin. Hours later, when he stirred from his postcoital doze, the scent seemed to have taken a deeper, almost caramelized quality. He touched her neck and shoulder with his lips and drank it in. She uttered a soft sound of content and turned to face him. The pillows and covers had miraculously retained their downy fluff, and it was heaven to feel one's solid mass by contrast moving under them.

"Hey," she whispered in the dark.

"Hey," he said in return, marveling at the hush which seemed to amplify the crisp rustle of the snowy bed linen.

"Hmmm—now I know why you brought me here," she murmured.

He said nothing, but pushed back her hair to cup her cheek

and reciprocate her kiss. When he pulled back, she traced a finger down the tip of his nose, then giggled and stretched her arms over her head.

"Forgot how much fun it was when we were trying," she said with a self-satisfied smile that Nolan heard more than saw.

He lay still, staring past her as she wrapped her arms around him and drew him close for another kiss. Her proximity and the intoxicating fragrance she gave off had all but drowned his sensibilities, and it would have been easy to close his eyes and drift off, except the word 'trying' kept pricking him like a chip of broken glass.

"Trying," he echoed, without turning it into a question. To do so would risk upsetting her, though he still wanted her to explain what she meant. The word was plain enough, but he refused to accept it.

"I know it's silly to call it magic, but—there's something about this place, you know? I'm sure we'll get it right this time," she sighed, as if she and Nolan were on the same page, and while he maintained a blank exterior, his thoughts spiraled down reiterations of: "What did you do? What did you do?"

His mind hopped back to the previous year and that winter morning when Emma had announced she was pregnant. The intervening weeks had mislead him into believing the unplanned-for conception had taken place sometime after the trip but now, a frantic retrospective calculation told him it was entirely possible (if not likely) that it had happened during their stay here. The room was pitch black, yet Nolan felt the need to close his eyes before asking, "Aren't you on the pill?"

After a searching pause, she simply said, "I don't have them."

"What do you mean you don't have them?"

"I didn't pack anything, remember? You were the one who packed everything for this trip."

"I know. And I did pack them, I know I did. I remember putting them in your toiletries bag with your toothbrush—" It struck Nolan then, the irony of contriving to erase all thoughts of pregnancy from her mind while still making sure she took measures to prevent it. And yet, did it not stop being a reminder once it became part of her daily routine, no different from medications and multivitamins?

His hand covered his face as he uttered a sound halfway between a resigned laugh and a groan. Here they were, two adults with an effective method of birth control between them, and they couldn't get it right! It reminded Nolan of a fellow teacher who fought the school board on the subject of providing female students' with contraceptives, arguing that, "you can't rely on men for that." Only this time he couldn't tell whether she was right or wrong. Nolan was dead certain he had packed her pills—he even recalled glancing over their number to see whether or not she required a refill. One doesn't plan a romantic weekend without considering what it entails and taking the necessary steps!

In the face of this slip, Nolan somehow managed to remain calm, though the effort was akin to stuffing a fast-inflating elephant into a locker. "It's fine. It's okay," he said emphatically. "We'll just have to make an appointment as soon as we get back."

"Why?" she said, though she had evidently guessed what was on his mind.

"Oh, honey. You know we can't—"

"Why not?" She sat up and spoke down to him, managing to sound both threatened and defiant. "Why can't we? Why else did we come here? We're not even sure if it happened—if it could…" Then, sounding like she was addressing herself, she vehemently added, as if trying to ward something off, "It did—it will—I'm sure of it!" Again, her tone shifted as she continued in a lowered voice. "I want this, Nolan. You don't understand, I want this so bad…"

Her voice failed her, and it was enough for Nolan to sit up and hold her only to be pushed aside. He tried to cover his awkwardness by fumbling for his glasses before turning the bedside lamp. On some level, he knew she would not respond to any overture until she felt heard and understood, but he struggled and fell short of finding the right words that would demonstrate that.

"Em, it's not that I don't understand," he began, hesitating a moment before taking the plunge. "We can't always have what we want no matter how much we want it. I remember as a boy wanting a dog so bad, only I couldn't have one thanks to my allergies," he concluded, thinking he had hit on a decent comparison.

Emma refused to look his way. "How could you compare a dog to a baby? Your own flesh and blood?"

"Okay, bad example, but… try to understand where I'm coming from." He sidled up to her, causing her to inch away. "Look, why are we arguing over this? We don't even know if anything's happened yet. Let's just make an appointment when we get home and see what the doctor has to say."

Emma knew what her husband really meant and tried to glare, but her round, wet eyes nullified the attempt, resulting in a look so plaintive it struck a blow to Nolan's heart. He reached his arm out, and this time Emma sullenly conceded to be held.

"You don't know," she said into his bare shoulder, warm breath misting his cool skin. "You don't know how long I've watched my friends announce their pregnancies and celebrate every milestone, sharing photographs and swapping stories… and I'm the only one there with nothing."

Nolan remained quiet, and perhaps reflecting on what she said, his wife added, "It's not just my friends. We don't feel like family when it's just the two of us. There's something missing—I feel it whenever you're out, or you're working late, and I'm sitting at home, watching TV or reading just to pass the time…"

There was an odd emphasis in the way she pronounced 'working late,' imbuing the words with a significance she thought he knew, except the hint was lost on Nolan.

"We could adopt, you know," he muttered against her head.

"I don't want to adopt," broke from her. "It wouldn't be fair. It wouldn't be the same. I want my own child—mine! Someone who's been a part of me from the start, someone who wouldn't grow up and leave me to go looking for his or her real parents."

"Em…"

"And I can do it! I know I can! The doctor said there was nothing wrong with me. Maybe I did something wrong. Maybe this time it'll be different. Maybe if I'm careful…"

Her voice broke, and Nolan felt compelled to detach himself a little, enough to align his face with hers.

"Hon, listen to me," he said firmly, "you can't keep doing this to yourself. You can't beat yourself over something beyond our control. I can't just sit by and let you torture yourself like this! We don't know if the doctor is right—that there's nothing wrong. Some things are simply not meant to be. And we just have to accept them and move on. You're not alone—you'll never be as long as I'm around. We *are* a family, you and I. I have everything I want right here. Why can't that be enough?"

She began to weep, and Nolan tenderly hushed her, resting his cheek on the top of her head as he stroked her back, partly wondering whether he managed to convince her, and at the same time ruminating on whether this ardent dream of hers would sustain itself on a desert island—whether she truly wanted it or merely coveted what her friends had. Would she really be happy with a baby, or was she fed this romantic notion of motherhood? As he absently kissed her sweet-smelling hair, his mind leapt onto an adjacent track, and he found himself questioning whether she was happily married to him, or was more in love with the idea of being married and would therefore be just as happy with someone else. The thought disturbed him, and he turned his head as if averting his gaze from an unpleasant sight, burying his face in her soft, fragrant locks. Meanwhile he continued to rock her gently like they did whenever they were slow dancing.

10

Nolan peered through the lobby window, estimating the hour. Nothing in the black sky indicated the time, nor did the lobby itself bear any time pieces for him to consult. His watch lay on the bedside table, but he was reluctant to go back upstairs and fetch it lest he disturbed Emma's troubled sleep. In the end it hardly mattered, the subject of time was little more than a stalling tactic meant to keep more troublesome questions at bay.

Did he do the right thing? It seemed sensible at the time, but now he almost marveled at the callousness it took to kill his poor wife's hope of having a baby. Yet how can it be callous when he wanted to spare her days or weeks of false hope that would in all likelihood lead to heartbreak? There was no dancing around the subject, and if there was a better way to put it, he lacked the time and forethought to compose a more delicate response. Even now he struggled to find the right answer, the type that would famously spring to mind long after the relevant conversation had ended.

Nolan's shoulder rested against the window panes, and the frosty air outside began to penetrate through glass and the fabric of his cotton wrapper. He stepped away from the window and sat hunched in one of the lobby sofas, resting his forehead on clasped hands. The dark and featureless lobby furnished a background for flashes of memories, and from that archive came a remembrance of that late night when Emma lay in a hospital bed, looking as wan and frail as the IV apparatus she was hooked to, her tearless eyes vacant and staring into the air. Hours had passed without them ever exchanging a word; the loss had struck them both, but if Nolan was heartbroken, it was for her sake. He remained by her side, both anticipating and dreading that moment when shock would subside and he would feel ineffective in the wake of unrelenting anguish. For better or worse, Emma remained in semi-catatonic state. A light had gone out of her, something beyond the sanguine radiance that for the past months had suffused her face with fruit-like color. Buried beyond Nolan's present recollection was a moment during his long vigilance in which he beheld his wife's haggard face and felt his heart overflow with tenderness. He lifted her hand and kissed it, then, finding that tribute lacking, rose and touched his lips to her clammy forehead.

Did he do the right thing?

They had struggled to conceive in the past, and he avidly hoped the odds were in his favor this time—that nothing would come of this slip. All the same, he made a mental note to visit the nearest drugs store for prophylactics or else fallback on other methods readily available if not quite as dependable. He reflected with some bitterness how couples who have no luck begetting children usually celebrated their newfound freedom, forgoing the cumbersome necessity of birth control. So what if her friends had babies and showers? All that celebration, to him, seemed like meager consolation in the face of all the looming burdens. What if motherhood was not the fulfilling dream Emma imagined it would be? What if her elation was short-lived once practical matters prevailed? What if they regretted the whole thing? What if his child was born with some congenital condition that requires medical attention beyond their financial capacities? What if they couldn't afford it? What if he was an inadequate father? What if he spoiled his child? What if he didn't love it enough? What if he did everything right and the child still didn't turn out good? His own students presented more than a few examples of that possibility—even those blessed with hardworking and attentive parents were not immune. Seen from that angle, the whole child-rearing enterprise felt like a walk in a minefield, and only the lucky few made it out intact. Not that Emma would see it that way, not when her friends hid the ugly parts and made motherhood to be this sunny, wholesome existence. Perhaps it was, and perhaps their marriage did lack something without children, but was it worth sacrificing the peace and stability they had in pursuit of her wants?

Had he done the right thing?

The question followed him as he rose from his seat and climbed the stairs, stopping short of gaining the upper landing. There he stood, listening for a sound that had almost disappeared before reaching his ears. It sounded like a choked cry, and with the events of the previous night still fresh in his memory, Nolan rushed to his room only to find Emma lying still in bed. Carefully he laid one hand on her shoulder, or rather brought it as close as he could without making contact, fearful lest his touch startled her; for the selfsame reason he refrained from reaching for the bedside lamp, relying on the whatever scant glow the dimly-lit hallway shed into their room. A few seconds passed with him continuing to scrutinize his wife's recumbent figure, sensing her breathing motions though never quite to his satisfaction, and while he was occupied so, he heard a muffled wail drifting down the hallway.

With only the three of them under one roof it required no process of elimination on Nolan's part to guess the source of the cry but that fact did not bring him any reassurance, nor did it make it easy for him to move from his spot. Emma was asleep, though she may as well have held him fast and kept him bound in place as she had done last night. He remained stooping over her long after the cry had died out, arms tingling with bristling hair like raised hackles.

Time crept on, and with it his fright began to ebb away. He began to feel annoyed, first with himself at being rattled so easily, then at the owner who seemed to disregard the fact she had guests sleeping a few doors down. As he went to close the door, he once again heard her raising a fresh lament, and suddenly felt a pang of concern. What could have made her so miserable that she would resort to this show of grief? Then it struck him that she might be suffering from a stroke or some similar affliction that required immediate attention. He hesitated, then without a second thought left his room and stole down the corridor.

On the way, he heard something slam a hard surface, like fists banging on a table, and again hesitated a moment. The noise directed him not to the master bedroom but to the room adjacent to it. Again he heard the fists pounding on the table, and over them she resumed her crying. It was a hideous sound. There is a form of weeping that is less wailing and more a choked sound, the type of crying displayed by very young children or grieving adults when they're all at once overcome with sorrow that in the midst of crying their throats seize up, the air flow is squeezed to a pinhole, and for a moment or two their mouths are open but the only sound passing through is a succession of ragged croaks.

Nolan stood listening outside the door. Any resolve he had of knocking on her door was slipping fast, more so when the wailing croaks unexpectedly broke into bouts of laughter. He stared opened eyed at the door, which even now was too thin a barrier between him and this unfathomable cacophony. What made it worse—if it even could be so—was the noise that accompanied it. The dull thumps returned with a vengeance, now sounding closer and clearer as sharp knocks, as of wood striking a wall. Another full-throated cackle came, louder and more strident than the first, petrifying Nolan into forgetting himself, insensible to the fact that he needed the support of the wall to remain on his feet.

He staggered backwards intending to beat a hasty retreat and in the process he collided with tall side table bearing a potted plant and toppled them over. A terrible silence followed the crash, or perhaps it seemed so to Nolan, whose mind had gone as blank as snow. Instantly he ran without heed to his room.

When he next came to his senses, Nolan found himself lying in bed next to Emma, his heart thumping against her back. In his haste to seek refuge, he had forgone the cumbersome labor of detangling the bedsheets to cover himself and now lay exposed to the chill air, cold sweat soaking his pajamas and thin cotton wrapper. Yet this minor oversight paled in comparison to a bigger blunder, which Nolan realized when the feeble lick of light from the hallway grew markedly dim.

Over his wife's shoulder, Nolan had a clear view of the vanity mirror and in it the reflection showed the doorway to their room, open and occupied by disheveled figure. There she stood, her entire front effaced by darkness, staring at them with eyes unseen.

11

"Nolan?"

The sound of his name broke the trance, and he found Emma eyeing him across the breakfast table at which he sat with fork and knife and a filled plate between them.

"You look like you're about to fall asleep," she said in answer to a questioning look he gave her.

Nolan failed to see how she got that impression when to him it felt like both eyes were incapable of blinking. He said nothing, putting down the silverware to pick up his cup of coffee. The liquid was cool to his lips, as though it had sat there for a while instead of minutes. All the same he drank it, grimaced over the bitter taste then poured himself a fresh cup, determined to remain alert for the long drive ahead.

"Already?" protested Emma when he told her they were to leave after breakfast. "Why?"

Nolan, avoiding her eyes, shrugged behind his lifted cup. "It's only a couple of hours ahead of check-out time," he said, not knowing what the hour was but hoping he was close-enough or that his wife would not notice the discrepancy.

She gave him a sad smile, somewhere between persuasion and a plea. "Why are we rushing? What's there to get back to? We still have the morning to ourselves. I'm sure Leah won't mind."

Nolan shook his head—not in response to Emma's proposal, but in reaction to Leah's name, the mere mention of which made him want to take his wife by the hand and lead her to the car. "You wouldn't want to stay here for a minute if you heard what I heard," he was tempted to say. Indeed, he came close to giving an honest answer before remembering the owner could be within earshot and instead he told her he had students' papers back home to go over and grade. "It's gonna be a long drive back—longer than coming here—maybe two hours. And we'll have to make a detour to stop for gas, you know…"

How easily he found all the right reasons for leaving early, which sufficed to convince Emma. She looked resigned and crestfallen, and her husband came close to saying, "It's only a few hours," except he realized the argument went both ways. Indeed, what's a few hours of isolated delight compared to an empty apartment and a mundane routine?

Would she understand, he wondered, if he told her the real reason they were leaving so early? Or would she dismiss it as an eccentric episode that did not involve them? With last night's events behind him and his departure approaching, it was hard not to consider the second view. Perhaps he was overreacting—perhaps the whole bizarre episode was nothing more than a vivid nightmare. His own feelings were nothing to go by, not when he has had dreams before in which he saw acquaintances who behaved in a way that had either stirred his affection or left him unreasonably surly and resentful. His sweat still had the singed odor of a spent fever, and he remembered the foraged mushrooms they had eaten for dinner, suspecting they played a role in what he saw—or thought he saw last night.

Nolan, eyeing the forkful of eggs which he had absently picked up, and which had bits of mushrooms in them, set the utensil down, transferring his wary glance to Emma's half-eaten omelet. He excused himself and left the breakfast table, half-pretending he was going upstairs to pack their things.

After their bags were packed and stowed in the car, Nolan stooped over the front desk to write a check for a sum that was surely greater than what he had paid last year.

It's the extra meals, he thought, as if trying to keep himself from arguing over the bill. Not that there was any risk of that when he avoided making eye contact with the owner, limiting himself to incidental glances. She too seemed quiet, though he felt her gaze fixed on him, as though she suspected something.

Did she catch sight of him last night, he wondered, a heavy nausea settling over him. It didn't matter—soon he'd be on his way and leave the entire unhinged incident behind. With palms prickling, he slid the signed check over to Leah, bade her good day, and turned to leave, still feeling her gaze following him.

In recent memory, nothing felt quite as reassuring as the brisk sound of the car door slamming shut. Nolan settled in the driver's seat, took a long breath and released it through a half-suppressed laugh.

Good riddance to this place!

The weekend had been an absolute disaster by almost every measure, save for the fact that Emma seemed to have shaken off her apathy.

"No matter," he said to himself, turning the key to start the car, "we'll go somewhere else." He went on thinking, pressing his lips while he turned the ignition key once more. "Some place better—somewhere new—and we'll make new memories…"

12

In the passenger seat, Emma turned from her pining contemplation of the bed and breakfast to watch her husband as he irritably turned the ignition key for the third then fourth unsuccessful time. He seemed uncharacteristically agitated, exiting the car to raise the hood and peer under it before slamming it down and plopping back in the driver's seat for more vain attempts at starting the car.

Emma went from sitting in the car to waiting in the lobby while her husband called roadside service and stood outside to flag them down. Leah, on finding Emma seated by the lobby window, invited her to have tea in her private room.

"Nolan asked me to wait here," she said.

Leah scoffed. "We're not going to the moon, lamb. You'll still be within shouting distance if anything happens." She took Emma's hand and led her upstairs before the latter had time to protest.

Five minutes later, over her steaming cup of tea, Emma said, "We're awfully sorry about all this."

"Nonsense," was Leah's affable answer. "It wasn't your idea to break the car down. And I expected you'd be spending the morning her before checkout. When Mr. May told me he wanted to settle the bill I said to him, 'You're not leaving already, are you?' but he didn't say anything. I haven't offended you in any way, have I?"

"No—no, you've been nothing but kind! It's just the long drive home, and he mentioned something about having work to do…"

"I see. Well, I hope you had a fine stay here. Celebrating your anniversary were you?"

"No."

"No? That's funny—I thought he… well, never mind."

"You thought he what?" Emma pursued.

"Nothing. Probably just the wine talking."

"Wine?"

"Drink your tea, lamb, there's a dear," said Leah in a languid attempt to dismiss the matter. When that failed she sighed and explained. "He said you were unhappy. He said it over dinner that first night. We were just having a conversation, that's all. But you know he was very shy at first, until he had a few glasses and then he became charming and talkative. I bet he's fun at social events."

"I guess so," said Emma, more to fill in the uncomfortable silence.

"I suppose he was making up for something."

"What?"

"You know—"Leah heavy lashes cast thick shadows, but Emma could see the subtle movement of the lids as her host lowered her eyes and rolled them to the side as if offering discretion from an unpleasant subject—"was he a naughty boy? Did you catch him making a pass at someone at a party or dipping into the neighbor's sugar bowl?"

Emma laughed in spite of herself. "No—no. He's not like that!" she said, and under Leah's persistent smile which seemed to challenge her to the contrary, she felt compelled to add, "Nolan's a good husband. He would never do anything like that."

Leah smiled. "Of course not, lamb."

"He's a good husband and a good man," Emma reassured her. "He takes care of things, even if he's been awful busy lately…"

"Busy with what?"

Emma's countenance clouded over with whirling thoughts. "Oh, you know," she said, catching one thread of thought and then just as quickly letting go, determined not to give in to petty jealousy. "Work and errands." She raised her gaze to find Leah regarding her with a touch of pity, a faint echo of yesterday's wretched look. The two of them had swiftly cultivated a bond over the past twenty-four hours, and while she wavered, Emma felt drawn to the strange woman who seemed to see through her cheerful facade, and pitied her.

"What does your instinct say?" inquired the older woman.

"I don't know," said Emma after pausing for what felt like a more than a minute.

"Men think logically, and they're good at covering their traces. That's why women have instincts. What does yours say?"

Emma dropped her gaze, almost ashamed. "It says that he's… drifting." She let the words play out behind her lips, refusing to grant them voice. It was one thing to talk about loss, but another thing entirely to acknowledge failure.

Leah startled her by clapping her hands together. "Mercy me, I didn't think I'd be filling your sweet little head with worries. Forget I said anything. I'm sure it's none of my business. I know I tend to get awfully nosy about things—and just as you're about to start home—as soon as your husband gets the car going. I hope nothing's wrong with it…"

"I hope so too," Emma absently agreed. "I mean I hope not! That is, I hope we'll be out of your way soon—you must have an awful lot to do taking care of the house all by yourself. There's two of us and we can barely manage a small apartment." Her self-critical laugh failed to move Leah, who only offered a tight smile while she listened. "Especially with all those plants," Emma went on, sensing her listener expected more from her. "How you manage to keep them all alive and healthy—"

"You've taken care of plants before?"

"No, not really. I tried taking care of a few ferns at work but they didn't last long. I guess I'm not good with—growing things," Emma concluded with a rueful drop of her voice.

Leah did not directly acknowledge this, but picked up a tiny spoon and began stirring her tea. "It's not about growing things so much as feeding them and letting them grow."

"If that's true, then I guess some things are not meant to grow." The admission upset Emma into setting her cup down with an abrupt gesture. She rose and turned away from her host, crossing her arms and tucking her cold hands under them. The resentment she harbored towards the owner's inquiry took an inwards turn, relentlessly poking into a still-gaping wound, and a nearby fresh one made by her own pecking thoughts.

"A man needs an anchor," is what Emma's mother often repeated—one of the many staid aphorisms that were largely ignored by her teenage daughter, who was just then discovering the art of hooking one. The same old adages returned to mock her now that her looks were fading and, with them, her husband's interest. A child would have indeed tethered Nolan to her, elevating their couple-hood into a family, and filling that hole in his heart that would inevitably lead him astray. Never mind that her husband expressed an aversion to the idea of starting a family—"men don't know their own minds," was another favorite of her mother's, usually muttered behind her husband's back after he ran in to ask her which tie he should wear before heading to work, leaving her to tend to their four kids.

Whether or not her mother had instilled domestic aspirations in her daughter was immaterial, since Emma herself had always cherished visions of a life revolving around a husband and children. Her average career achievements only bolstered the notion that she was made for that life. She could keep a job but never aspired to a career, dreaming instead of a perfect home in the suburbs that would house a happy family, going as far as to hope her grown children would follow in her steps and marry young to provide her with grandchildren to fill in for them.

"Useless, useless, useless old bag!" Emma inwardly jeered, having been raised to believe that any achievement was within hand as long as she worked hard for it and wanted it badly enough while having to contend with every disadvantage known to woman. The maddening question was what did she have to do and who did she have to convince to be able to get what she most wanted?

Emma heard Leah behind her, setting her cup down with a quiet clink. By then, the worst of Emma's frustration had boiled over and began to subside, and in its place stole a mild sense of embarrassment. She turned to face the owner, partly-expecting an apology for delving into a sensitive subject. Instead, she found Leah standing before a chest of drawers, the type containing dozens of small, square compartments, opening and closing drawers in random sequence before it became apparent that she was pulling out something and passing it to the other hand to hold.

The sight arrested Emma until an insect flew by and alarmed her into looking its way. It settled on a flower of a nearby potted plant, and Emma saw that it was a black bee with iridescent blue wings, spread and poised for instant take off. In fact, the neighboring flowers had similar visitors as well, some climbing up and down a cluster of yellow foxgloves, others making a brief dive into the petaled shafts before flying off.

All at once the bees scattered and disappeared, as if suddenly frightened, and a moment later, Emma felt something pressed into her hand. "Put this under your husband's pillow," Leah said. "It's to help keep your marriage. This will bind your husband to you."

Emma kept her hand held out, neither accepting this gift nor rejecting it, though she was inclined to the latter. A faint dry odor wafted from the tiny bundle, and the longer she looked, the more the threads appeared to resemble long strands of hair. She knew of spells and charms, remembered the craze that swept her all-girls middle school, and the youth pastor's stern warning against them. Back then the spells involved chants, candles, and names hidden in triple folded papers—all things which Emma nervously dabbled in once and was half-disappointed and half-relieved to discover they were ineffectual. Over the years, fears of hellfire and eternal damnation had long faded, but traces of them apparently lingered in her psyche.

"It's just that—I'm not sure if it'll work…" she trailed off, transfixed by the long look Leah gave her, as though she was about to divulge a confidential matter.

"I saw a vision last night," she began, "of an infant standing outside my room. It signed me to follow, and I did until it lead me to your room."

Emma forgot about the bundle cradled in the palm of her hand and stared the owner's parched face as she continued. "It wanted me to open the door—kept pointing at it as if it expected me to let it in. I still see it now. And when I woke up, I found myself standing in front of your room, and the door was wide open."

Color and heat suffused Emma's face, not a blush of embarrassment but of secret fervor. She blinked once or twice before she spoke. "I don't understand. Was it a dream? What does it mean?"

Instead of answering, Leah caught Emma in a whimsical embrace, jolting the latter into closing her hand over the tied bundle. Still holding her close so that the sound seemed to vibrate through, the older woman murmured, "She wants to be born."

13

The morning passed without anyone ever showing up. Nolan remained obstinately posted by his car, ready to flag down any vehicle with a phone number stenciled on its side. He called the same number once before lunch and again soon after, but no one picked up.

Clouds began to gather by early afternoon, and soon after the refreshing breeze turned into a driving gust, stripping trees of their brown foliage and carrying off light debris. Around that time the phone rang from roadside service.

"Can't make it today. Bad weather. Might not look it now, but there's a storm coming. Too risky to drive all the way there. You're not stuck in the middle of the road, are you? Good—I'd stay put if I were you. I'm sorry but that's just how it is. Suit yourself, but I'm guessing you won't find any cabs now."

After trying the local cab companies without success, Nolan called the school and left a message saying he wouldn't be able to come in on Monday. At that moment, Emma happened to be descending the stairs, and from the way she paused before the last few steps with a poorly hidden smile, Nolan could tell she had overheard him and was delighted about their extended stay.

"Leah said we're welcome to spend another night here, if we want."

There was something funny with that clause, 'if we want,' as if the matter was up to them. Nolan sighed and reached out to take one of Emma's hands, finding fugitive comfort in her happiness and the way her fingers lay in his. He himself was not happy with the arrangement, but what could he do besides sleeping in the car or braving the coming storm on foot for miles and miles in search of shelter elsewhere? On reflection, he had to concede that—apart from the weather—the day had been relatively peaceful and though his wife went against his wishes and sat upstairs with the owner, no harm seemed to have come to her.

"Well, you got what you wanted," he said, drawing her close. "Now what?"

Her proximity reminded him of the last time they went dancing, though for the past few years their range in that department had been reduced to slow numbers. The diminishment was welcome on Nolan's side, and he suspected Emma did not entirely miss those awkward moments when he was chaperoning school dances and would be urged by enthusiastic students to show his moves, oftentimes with humorous results. It was the same custom year after year, but Nolan took the short-lived humiliation with affable grace, smiling at himself and granting that his students deserved to catch a break and laugh with (if not at) their teacher. Emma would often attend such events with slightly more energy than him, to the point where Nolan wondered whether she relived her own high school experience vicariously through them. He himself remembered their first slow dance, how their faces hovered close, how the tip of his nose would brush against hers, sending a sympathetic sweep rushing down the back of his neck. Back then, it wouldn't have taken much to send him over the edge, but he wanted to linger and drink up this sublime state of in-between, so he closed his eyes, dissociated from that part of him that wanted more, felt all the more weightless for it, and floated off as if carried by a gentle current.

They never made much of their weekend, and despite his nagging unease, he wanted to put aside the troubling episode and enjoy Emma's returning good humor.

Emma, perhaps guessing what was on his mind, lifted her hands and took off his glasses. Behind them were thin eyebrows and eyes with tapered corners that gave him a sharp look, though such details were lost thanks to the diminishing effect of a large frame and concave lenses. Years ago, when his glasses broke and he had brought her along to help him select a new pair, she convinced him that rimless glasses made him look timid and effete, while the dowdy, oversized frames bestowed him with a professorial look and old school gravitas befitting a teacher.

Timid and effete were all Nolan needed to hear to make his decision—he was inclined towards the first pair until Emma hit on the two words he least wanted associated with him. The large glasses was a new look to Nolan, but he took his wife's advice in good faith, missing the salesman's doubtful side glance over Emma's remarks—so much so that he held on to them, even when the bridge of the glasses broke and had to be taped together, and he was genuinely grateful when Emma got him a similar pair for his birthday. Any opposing opinion, especially in the form of a comment made by a fellow male teacher, only served to cement Nolan's view that a single man's taste is a different breed and sometimes all the poorer in its unmitigated state, and if the commenter happened to be anyone other than a bachelor, Nolan shrugged it off, saying that in the end taste was subjective. Never once had he suspected Emma's true motive behind her choice—that she hoped the unattractive glasses would ward off unwanted attention. However there was no mistaking her candid delight in removing his glasses during their intimate moments, which Nolan equated with the secret thrill he felt whenever Emma untied her hair and bend over to shake the waves loose.

With that image in mind, he obediently followed as she took him by the hand and led him upstairs.

The wind whistling outside perforated through Nolan's rest that night and kept him in a troubled state between wakefulness and sleep. Though the noise sometimes furnished a source comfort to the sheltered listener, presently it worried his slumber to tatters and jarred his nerves whenever the whistle rose to a thin shriek, until he lay with closed eyes unable to sink back into dreams.

A light doze washed over him, and when it ebbed away he was aware that the wind had died out. The quiet was such that he heard the phone ringing somewhere in the distance below, echoing like it came from a great black chasm. It rang a few times, faint yet clear, then it too fell silent, and the ensuing hush settled over Nolan like fresh snow. But it was a peace he could not trust, and while his open eyes plumbed the murky stillness, he strained to listen from the relative safety of his bed for any disturbance in the hallway, reassured by the certainty that the door to their room was locked.

For a spell he lay so, going as far as to suspend his breathing, reckoning that as soon as he relaxed, the awful clamor would begin. But nothing was heard beyond the locked door, while near him Emma's soft, regular breathing served to ease his mind. By degrees, his attention shifted to that almost imperceptible whistle of air as she inhaled and then just as softly exhaled. Relief overcame him in the form of a slight shiver, which gladly did not disturb the sleeper next to him.

Through the walls he heard the rush of running water, and a few seconds later the bathroom door opened, dousing the bedroom with bright yellow light. In the illuminated rectangle of the doorway stood the hazy yet familiar form of his wife.

"Oh," she said, surprised to find him sitting up in bed. "I'm sorry. Did I wake you up?"

Her husband did not answer, but sat up staring at the empty spot next to him in bed.

14

Nolan woke up the next morning with a wince and began to cough. Something was lodged in the back of his mouth, and before he had a chance to shake off the drowsiness, he stuck a forefinger and thumb into his mouth and fished out a wet clump of what felt to be hair. The sensation was vile enough for him to immediately toss it to the floor, wiping his hands on his pajama trousers before reaching for his glasses.

It was indeed a clump of black hair which Nolan picked off the floor with the tips of his fingers. He felt sick to his stomach, but thankfully the nausea did not express itself past a grimace of disgust as he carried the offensive thing to the trash bin.

The incident robbed Nolan of his appetite, leading him to shun breakfast and limiting himself to coffee and drinking it with the steam still rising if just to scald away that lingering ghost of hair tickling the inside of his throat.

"Now I know what a cat feels like," he muttered, pouring himself a fresh cup.

Emma looked up from the slice of toast she was spreading with jam. "What feels like a cat?"

Nolan started to elucidate but thought better of it: the subject was not one for the breakfast table. Besides, the analogy was inaccurate given that the clump was not made up of his hair—nor his wife's for that matter. Only one head in this house possessed hair of that color, though it did not begin to explain how it ended up in his mouth, unless he considered the possibility of ingesting it through the food she prepared. He entertained the theory for a protracted second before dismissing the entire subject with a head shake.

"Road Assistance better show up today," he said, swallowing another scorching draft.

Emma nodded with downcast eyes, more to humor him than in agreement, and did it with such an air of forbearance that it provoked Nolan into adding, "You know I was supposed to be at school today," if just to remind her that it wasn't his idea to end their extended stay.

"I know," she sighed, sounding half-apologetic. "But wouldn't it be nice if…"

"If?"

"If you didn't have to go to work, you know? If we just woke up, got dressed and came downstairs for breakfast, and then just went to work here—running the place, you know?"

"What's wrong with going to work?"

"Nothing," she rejoined, a little impatient at his missing the point. "I just think it would be nice to run a business from home where we can be together all day."

Nolan pursed his lips while he considered, guessing she aspired to run her own bed and breakfast, and hoping it would push aside other unattainable ambitions. "I suppose we could do that. Maybe fifteen or twenty years from now."

"Fifteen years?" she protested.

"Well—it's not like we have enough to make an investment like this—unless we get some kind of windfall or something. In the meantime, we'll just have to save up, maybe wait for the next recession to find a good deal on a house."

The prospect did not appear promising to Emma, who continued to look despondent. "This house sure felt like home," she murmured.

Instead of remarking, Nolan returned to his original subject. "If RA don't show up, I'll have to call a cab and a car towing service." He set down his cup and slipped his fingers behind his glasses to rub his eyes when a hand perched on his shoulder.

"Did I hear you right, Mr. May?" said Leah with mildness meant to downplay the abrupt clasp. "You wish to have your car towed?"

She stood behind him while she spoke, reeking of that old, cloying fragrance that still failed to cover the sulfurous fumes. Nolan's first instinct was to peel the hand off his shoulder, but he managed to transpose his intention into a reassuring pat.

"We've imposed on you long enough," he said, laying his hand on Leah's without meeting her eyes. "You were very kind to let us stay one more night."

"Think nothing of it," she replied, laying a second hand on his in counter-reassurance. "I was just wondering why the driveway was empty this morning. I suppose they must have removed it already."

Nolan was forced to look up at her, if just to search for hints of a joke. His rush from the dining room was followed by the crash of his chair toppling over, and he skidded to a halt before the lobby's window, still entertaining a wild notion that this was Leah's idea of a joke, only to discover the large vista of front yard and driveway did not include his car. His subsequent dash threatened to upset a dainty legged plant display, but in four seconds flat Nolan stood outside to confirm what he had already established but vehemently denied—the car was gone.

In the center of the gravel sweep he stood, looking for tire tracks, loose gravel or any telling signs of disturbance in the leaf-strewn driveway. His survey quickly proved futile, and Nolan reentered the house to call roadside assistance. No one picked up, and after a long inner debate, he dialed the number of a local cab company, determined to go there himself.

It bothered him to see Emma's mournful face when he told her they were leaving as soon as their cab arrived, but what he took for sadness was in fact concern over his appearance.

"Honey, please sit down," she said, rising from her seat to guide him and using a soft conciliatory tone he had not heard in a while. "Sit down and eat something—you look like you're ready to drop."

Nolan insisted he was fine but nevertheless took a seat. "Just get the bags, please. We don't want to keep the cab waiting," he said, burying his face in his hands and inadvertently pushing his glasses up, glad to be able to get the sentence out before his rising gorge got the better of him. He remained in that attitude, determined to shut everything out until the cab arrived (or else he gained better control over his stomach) before remembering he still had a bill to settle.

His displaced glasses fell when he lowered his hands to reach for the checkbook in his jacket's inner pocket, and he presently groped for them, closing his eyes against the sudden wave of vertigo and hoping no one noticed the beads of sweat straining through every pore. Up until then he had told himself that this was nothing more than an onset of fatigue, ignoring the uncoiling ache of his insides that argued otherwise. He would feel right soon—or as soon as he got into the gentle roll of a car driving him and Emma back home. He still had to call for a cab...

The infernal glasses had apparently fallen to the floor, and Nolan's increasingly heavy pats were perforce carried down to reach for them. But the shift proved precarious, and soon the rest of him followed as he tipped over, dragging the tablecloth down with him.

15

Through wavering awareness Nolan's mind swam, registering his wife's indistinct features and touch as she held his clammy face, pressed a hand to his forehead and cried, "Poor Nolan! Oh, poor baby!" before sinking into blackness. His breathing was shallow, his pulse swift, but faster yet was the comings and goings of footsteps and movement around him as he lay in bed, the motions of heads and hands blurred in their speed, as though spurred by the same simmering fever.

Through parted lips billowed the furnaced air, barely allowing Nolan to draw in cooling breath. He made no complaint save for the occasional involuntary groan culminating the worst of his shivering.

Throughout this his mind kept returning to that moment when his wife held his face, the hazy memory itself carrying scant significance. Yet his mind fixed on it, behaving like a maddening individual who kept showing the same photo over and over. Again and again he saw her face floating nebulously over his, though each revisit seemed to eliminate one muddy feature after another, save for the crescentic row of white teeth lined up in a smile.

When he opened his eyes again it was to a world of dimmed light and stillness, and an unrecognizable figure sitting in a chair near the head of the bed.

"Who are you?" Nolan meant to say, but found himself incapable uttering more than a weak moan.

Somehow the seated stranger understood and leaned in, bringing his face close. "Can you see me?" he asked.

Nolan's eyes made a minute sideways flick to encompass the swathe of dark features floating close. He blinked, nodded, and the man's face wrinkled into a benign smile. He drew back, and the face reverted to its amorphous state.

"Let's get started," he said, rising to his feet, and without further ado began using the heel of his hands to apply pressure in firm upward strokes, pushing Nolan's tender stomach further into his ribs. The motion and force was like a thumb pushing the last bit of paste out of a tube, and Nolan had the sickening sense his guts were crowding his lungs. Before long, before he had a chance to protest or tell the man to stop, he rolled over and emptied his stomach.

The noise summoned Emma to his side, ready with soft words and cool hands, using the latter to feel Nolan's head and cheeks while she hushed and soothed, though he did not fret or fuss.

"It's all right," she said in a sunny drawl, stepping back to fetch a wet cloth, wringing it over a basin before using it to wipe Nolan's face. "There, now. That's better. Just lie back and rest. I'll get something to clean it up."

She disappeared through the door, and the man seated at the bedside leaned in for a second look.

"You live here?" he said, pulling down one of Nolan's eyelids.

Little as he saw, Nolan marked the pensive frown corrugating the man's brows. "We're just guests here."

His listener's frown relaxed into an expression which Nolan could not read but heard it in his stony reply.

"Leave, then. You've overstayed your hospitality."

Before he knew what he was doing, Nolan caught the man by his wide-mouthed sleeve and noticed the man wasn't wearing a shirt, but a long white robe with an open collar. This hardly fazed Nolan, and he went on to say, "Call us a cab. Please."

The man stood, unhindered by the clutch on his sleeve. Nolan's eyelids slid heavily down. He blinked and rolled his eyes trying to get them to open again. For a moment he thought the man had disappeared, but no—there he stood, though the outline of his form oscillated and grew less coherent. Watching him hurt Nolan's eyes and brought on a headache that made him sick again. Not much came out, though once again Emma was there at his side to rub his back until he rolled over to his side.

"Em," he plaintively called.

She bent towards him to answer. "I'm here."

"What's wrong with me? What did the doctor say?"

The tremble in his voice moved her to draw the blanket over him, though she paused at the second question. "Doctor?"

"There was a man here—wearing white. He was trying to examine me."

Emma studied him for a moment, then sat on the edge of the bed. "No one was here," she tentatively said, smoothing back his ruffled hair.

So exhausted was he—so full of a latent self-pity—that even if he tried to argue he knew it was a waste of energy. Instead, he closed his eyes, yielding to the implication that he dreamt the whole thing, letting Emma run one hand over his head while his icy fingers curled over the other.

The faint clatter of a bucket being lifted roused Nolan into tentatively opening one eye, catching sight of Emma's clouded form as she stood from kneeling on the floor, where she had evidently been scrubbing. Minutes must have gone by since he passed out as the light from the window was still the same dull gray of an overcast morning, and the acrid air of vomit was masked by the sharp scent of vinegar.

A throbbing pain made him close his eye for a few moments, opening it again to the sound of whispers. The details and fine lines were lost to him, but his eyes managed to track his wife as she moved towards the foot of the bed, where Leah stood. He lost sight of them when an encroaching headache forced him to close his eyes again.

For an indeterminate time he swam in and out of consciousness, now and then opening his eyes for a few seconds in hopes of keeping track of time or of movement around him. Wan daylight diminished and was soon replaced by a sallow-hued ceiling light. Through heavy lids he saw a shadowy outline that was hard to make out without straining his eyes. Just the same, he knew it was Emma from her perfume when she came close enough and laid a cool hand on his forehead and cheek, feeling his temperature. The result must have been reassuring, as afterwards she readjusted the bed covers, then leaned down and kissed his head, near the hairline. So softly did the skimming lips lay their pressure that he couldn't help the tribute of a faint sound, somewhere between a sigh and a moan, before noticing as she stepped back that her hair was all black and the golden halo surrounding her was really that of the ceiling light shining behind her.

16

A warm lick across his stomach startled Nolan out of sleep. His eyes flew open the same instant he seized the wrist of the intrusive hand that was smearing something over his middle. In his panic-stricken state, and in the paltry light of the bedside lamp, it took him some time to recognize the semi-distinct figure whose hand he held as that of his wife. Still he stared at her, holding her hand by the wrist as if it had a knife meant to disembowel him. Why he held her so—what made him pant and sweat like someone delivered fresh from a nightmare, he could not say. All he could do was catch his breath, aware she was likely reciprocating his wide-eyed stare.

After he grew calm enough to let go of her hand, Emma showed him the salve she had brought to rub on his stomach, hoping to ease his pain and help him sleep better. Nolan brushed her off, more concerned with the fact that his clothes were gone. He remembered relinquishing his jacket and shoes before getting into bed, though he retained most of his day clothes, determined to leave as soon as he felt well enough to climb into a cab—even if the idea of a long car ride daunted him.

"We had to wash them," she told him, laughing a little the way she would over a slight mishap. "It was a struggle taking them off, you wouldn't let go of your blanket. Aren't you comfortable like this? I hear it's good for regulating your temperature. I think it helped too—the fever did go down. Leah made this salve and told me to—"

While she spoke, Nolan lay his heavy head down, meaning to ask her to fetch his clothes and call for a cab, but the panic episode had sapped what little energy he had stored up and he soon drifted off.

Even while he slept, his mind remained vigilant, enough to register the sensation of hands laid on his stomach. Half-awake now, he assumed that Emma was applying the salve as she said she would, only he wondered why a strange chant was involved in the process. The intoned words were half-intelligible syllables, but understanding them took a backseat to the uncomfortable sensation of his stomach as it rose and fell under their interlaced fingers, then rose again in a swell, drawing the skin tight and straining it until his middle burst into a glorious mound of mushrooms.

Up he bolted with faint frantic yelps, clutching the duvet to soak the blood. His quick breathing did not slow, not even after the limp cover gave no hint of dampness besides that of perspiration. Nolan took stock of his dark surroundings, felt the bed to make sure it was there and that he had it to himself. If he felt relieved, it was colored by wariness and the bewildered sense that Emma should have been here. Then it occurred to him that she was probably sleeping in another room, though he was too weak to get up and verify the fact. He lay curled on his side, on guard against anything that might upset his stomach, and began to wonder whether he suffered from food poisoning or a sudden onset of stomach flu. Towards dawn he began to nod off, only to jerk awake again when Leah barged in.

"I brought you something to drink," she announced, setting a small tray with a glass of murky liquid on the bedside table near him.

Nolan ducked for cover under the blanket and gave her a hoarse thanks meant to dismiss her though she would hear none of it.

"You have drink it now to settle your stomach. Otherwise you won't be able to keep anything down."

"Just leave it there and I promise you I'll drink it," came his answer from under the blanket.

After a pause she said, with a sly note that was somehow worse than her severe tone, "Oh, come now—you're not shy, are you? Why, we're hardly strangers at this point."

Afraid she was going to elaborate—or worse, fling the linen to one side—Nolan emerged from under the covers, and found himself having trouble sitting up without something to keep him propped. All this he did with his eyes closed to minimize the likelihood of vertigo, so that it surprised him to feel hair brushing against his face, and shrank when he realized Leah was leaning over him to adjust the pillows behind his head.

Without intending to, his eyes lit on the gap made by the slacking collar of her dress, which ranged close enough to the point where his vision was sharp and clear. Was it deepening shadows he saw, or did he glimpse glossy black hair covering her skin? It was but a brief glance, but what little he saw suggested an abundance of short dense hair like that of animal hide. His reaction betrayed nothing as he remained frozen in place until she drew back.

"Is everything all right?"

The query sailed past Nolan who was still questioning what he saw, attributing it to a trick of light and shadow, even if a trace of shine on that dark hair was burnt in his mind. But if he could not trust his eyes, could he likewise discredit his nose when it picked up a pungent odor peculiar to goats?

"Is everything all right, Mr. May?"

"I'm fine," he answered automatically, almost sounding out of breath. The answer nevertheless satisfied Leah, who proceeded to pick up the glass and bring it close to his face. Nolan instinctively pushed it aside, and the back of his hand registered the frosty touch of glass, indicating it was left to sit for hours in the fridge.

"You want to get better, don't you?" she argued. "This will put you right. You'll be on your feet in no time."

"What's in it?"

"Boiled herbs help settle your stomach. Now drink."

She lifted a glass to his lips. This time the strong stench struck him and he shied his head away, but the glass remained firmly held in place.

"Drink it quickly, in one go," she urged, cupping his chin to keep him still as she tipped the cold brew to his mouth. Her grip was surprisingly strong, or else he was more drained than he imagined—whatever the case was, she managed to force him to down his drink. The metallic bitter taste paled in comparison to its potent smell, which swamped him even as he held his breath and swallowed it in strained gulps—small mercy that the glass was short and the ordeal brief.

"There now," she said in a brighter voice, tilting his head back to make sure he drank it to the last drop.

Nolan waited for the wave of nausea to subside before asking where Emma was. He squinted at the bedside table but could not find his glasses.

"Your angel is making you soup," answered Leah, taking glass and tray and heading to the door. "Thanks to my medicine, you'll be able to keep it down instead of splashing it all over the carpet."

17

It was hard to tell whether the brew was truly meant to settle his stomach or whether it was a soporific. Hours later, when Nolan woke up from a dreamless sleep, he found that his body had sweated out the fever, and he sat up, measuring his capability of remaining vertical unassisted. So far, the result was encouraging—he felt lighter in spite of body aches and a general residual weakness.

Mellow daylight filled the room, brightening the tangle of flowers on the walls, but his glasses were still nowhere to be seen. He gave up trying to find them and ventured out of bed and into the bathroom for a quick shower, managing one without incident. Then, while he slipped on one of the guests bathrobes, Nolan heard a crash and saw that he had knocked over one of the many plants lining the sink counter.

For a moment he stood frozen, staring at the abstract mess of plant, soil and clay. Then, without taking time to think it through, he stooped down and rescued the plant, placing it in the sink bowl as a sort of transitional pot before going back to scrape up the soil. Knowing little about plants, Nolan had the naive impression that like fish they're liable to choke and die if left outside their natural element for as little as a minute, and in the process of gathering the scattered soil, he kept questioning his course of action even while he had accumulated a small mound of dirt and was sticking the plant into it.

His heart gave a brief stutter when he heard a tap on the door.

"Nolan, are you in there?" called Emma's voice.

"Yeah," he called back, and was about to wash his hands when he remembered the plant sitting there.

"I have your glasses with me. Can I come in?"

Nolan, after a short and hopeless survey, opened the door and showed Emma the mess on the floor.

"I'm willing to pay for it," he said, looking sheepish.

His wife merely shrugged and said she would clean it up. She gave Nolan his glasses before taking the plant downstairs to be repotted. Nolan then stooped down to pick up the last of the broken pieces. Amongst the clay shards, he found a yellowish gray fragment the size and width of which almost covered his pointer and middle finger together.

It was a bone fragment, of that Nolan was almost certain: there was no mistaking the color and texture. He raised his head to scan the surrounding plants, as if trying to divine whether below the soil their roots twined over similar pieces. His circling gaze reached the bathroom door, and he was startled to find Emma standing there with the silent air of observation, as though on the watch for something.

"I brought you some soup," she said with a sidestep meant to coax him back to bed.

Nolan obeyed, following her in a daze until she had him sitting up with pillows at his back and the bed tray set before him. It was then that he showed her the bone fragment and watched as she frowned over the shard resting in her palm.

Her conclusion was summed up in a careless shrug, much like the one she gave over the broken planter. "So?"

"So?" echoed her husband. "What do you mean 'so?' Don't you find that weird?"

"Honey, it's just a bit of bone."

"So what's it doing hiding in a potted plant?"

"You're asking me?"

"No, Em. I'm showing it to you 'cause I think something is really off here. This place—this house. The owner—" he continued through her short incredulous laugh— "I don't think she's right."

"You don't think she's right?" repeated Emma with lingering humor meant to reflect the absurdity of his claim. "And this is your proof?" she added, lifting her hand to indicate the fragment.

"That's not it," he began. "She's just weird. She... I heard her crying the other night. Crying and laughing at the same time."

"When was that?"

"The other night," he repeated, growing frustrated with his failing memory and his wife's incredulity. "That night before the day we were going to leave. But even this—" He snatched the bone fragment to hold it up. "How do you explain this? Why is this hidden in a plant pot?" He glanced at the door before leaning in to continue in a lower voice. "I'll tell you why: bones are the hardest thing to destroy. You can't burn them, you have to dissolve them in acid. But if you don't have that, and you don't want to bury them in your backyard where someone can dig them up, you break them into bits and hide them in plants cause no one would think to look there."

The illness had taken the ruddiness out of his complexion, leaving him with little color to show when Emma doubled over with laughter.

"What if I told you there's a perfectly good explanation for this?" she said, reclaiming the fragment and cradling it in her hand like a seashell. She stretched her dramatic pause a beat or two, perhaps granting Nolan time to guess what was on her mind. "Honey, she uses bones in her cooking. That's how we made the soup. You chop some carrots, celery, and onions, and you toss them into a pot of seasoned water with some chicken bones. You let it simmer for a few hours, then strain the liquid. I don't think I've ever seen anyone preparing it from scratch. I thought everyone just heated it up from a can, like my mother used to do. Anyway, so after it's all done, and I was about to throw away the scraps when she told me to set them aside to throw into the compost heap. It's these special drawers where she stores almost all kinds of food wastes: peels, eggshells, coffee grounds—bones."

"She stores scraps in the kitchen drawers?" Nolan concluded with a note of skepticism.

"Not in the kitchen, in the cellar! She's even got worms in there, eating away at everything and breaking them down into soil for the plants. This piece of bone must have come from there."

"And you've seen this compost heap of hers?"

Emma wrinkled her nose in a slight grimace that might have been disinterest or disgust. "It's not the type of thing I want to see. I just listened to her explain it to me while we were in the kitchen. She was showing me how she prepared leftovers for the compost heap. She even taught me how to turn eggshells into powder to protect your home—"

"So, you haven't seen it."

His wife's rising enthusiasm ebbed away, and she regarded him with a look of frank boredom. "No, I haven't."

"Did she offer to show it to you?"

"What difference does it make?" said Emma, trying to cover her exasperation with a chuckle.

"Of course she's happy to tell all about it, as long as she doesn't have to show it to you—not when she's hiding something down there."

He was in earnest, though Emma received this like a joke that was fast becoming tired. "I don't know what you have against her but I think you're making a skeleton out of an old t-bone."

"You didn't see what I saw," Nolan almost said, but held back, recognizing the flimsiness of his counterargument, and so begrudgingly fell silent and picked up the spoon to start on the soup. After all, of the two of them, his wife spent more time with the owner, granting her several chances to mark any strange behavior. Kind-hearted as Emma was, she prided herself on possessing instincts sharp enough to see through a false facade, and would not be fooled into trusting a person if she sensed something was off. Moreover, he had to remind himself that it was not evidence he was following, but a faulty notion born from one night's event—one that played out like a bad dream, though sometimes dreams have a stronger hold on one's mind than reason.

"I called the school, by the way," Emma went on, brightening a little, "to tell them you weren't feeling well."

"You didn't have to," he said between spoonsful, "I feel better now."

"No, but listen—the school secretary said it's all the same because school's closing early today. Seems there's been an outbreak of mumps at school. She said school will be out for the remainder of the week—maybe even two weeks."

"Wait—hold on. There's been a what now?"

"An outbreak of mumps—at your school."

"Who told you that?"

"I told you, it was the secretary—I forget her name. Anyway, I called to tell her you're not feeling well, and that you had a high fever, and she said, 'Are you sure it's not the mumps?' and I said, 'No, I don't think so,' and she said that a lot of the students and even a couple of teachers seem to have it, so starting tomorrow they're closing the school."

This breathless delivery puzzled Nolan almost as much as the news itself. He knew there was no reason to repudiate her report, only the matter was so sudden and extraordinary that hearing it secondhand roused the skeptic in him.

"At least you don't have to worry about attending if everyone's off for now," she continued with averted eyes, unable to suppress a guilty smile. "You can take your time to rest and recover…"

Nolan understood where this was going long before she uttered the second part, but he had yet to recover from the unexpected news to form an intelligent response. The situation was surreal enough to make him doubt it was taking place outside a vivid dream. Practical concerns prevailed, and through them he found his way back into the conversation.

"Honey, we've already stayed longer than we planned. It's not that I... I don't want to make it about money, but we can't afford to stay. We got a long cab ride back home—plus we still need to get the car—"

"But, Nolan, that's the best part! Leah said it's all right. We can stay for almost no cost—"

"And what does 'almost no cost' exactly mean?"

She smiled and took his hands as if bracing him for overwhelming news. "I decided to apprentice here."

"Apprentice? What do you mean apprentice? Apprentice for what?"

"For running a bed and breakfast. It's our dream, isn't it?" she hurried to add. "I told Leah about it and she offered to let us stay and learn in exchange for help—you know, chores and such. We lived in an apartment most of our lives, we don't know the first thing about running a house, let alone taking care of guests. There's so much we could learn from her."

It was his turn to laugh. "Learn what? We're her first guests!"

"Please, Nolan," she said, squeezing his hands, one of which still held the soup spoon. "There's nothing to go back to. I mean, there's no reason to rush home. You've got time off and Leah offered to let us stay. I could learn so much in a few days. And I don't mind the chores—really, I don't. So why not make the most of it?"

Nolan found better expression in a snort of derision than to say, "I know there's going to be a catch somewhere!" Yet, he could not deny that it made more sense to stay here and try to get his car back instead of taking a cab for the long drive home.

His disgruntled acceptance earned him an unexpected kiss, which Emma delivered with enough force to surprise Nolan, as though she was trying to shut him up—only he did not see it like that. Or rather the part of him that might have seen it that way was losing grounds to other parts that responded to that kiss. She drew back an inch but only to give him a second one, then a third or more—his mind stopped counting beyond four—'til he was far gone by the time she pulled back, cupped his slack jaw, thumbing the bony line while his mouth began to close then dropped open again.

Should she drag him down and drown him in molasses, he would not fight it.

18

Early that evening, Nolan stole downstairs to the reception area to make a few calls. At this hour, he doubted anyone would pick up at school, and indeed no one did. He hung up the phone and began dialing the number for road assistance.

How many days has it been? How many more days will they spend here? As an agreement won through attrition gains but a precarious seat, the idea of their protracted stay did not sit well with Nolan. He suspected some of the details of their free stay were slurred or unstated—that Emma had overestimated the owner's generosity, who perhaps meant she would let them stay for free while plying them with hidden charges. It seemed odd to Nolan that Emma was fixated with the idea of running a bed and breakfast, but upon consideration he supposed she had merely found a suitable substitute for dreams of starting a family. He wondered now whether she would just as summarily toss away any notion of running her own establishment if they were to go back home and she returned to her social circle with their pregnancy announcements and baby showers. Dream for dream, he would rather have her chase the more attainable one, even if it took them years of scrimping and saving.

The receiver was still in one hand and he was halfway through dialing, arrested by the last two thoughts. Why the rush indeed when they were happy—or at least his wife was—right where they were? After all, if their car was towed away, all it took was a call to have it brought back. Who else would have bothered to remove it if not road assistance? Thus went the line of his inner thoughts, yet it was as if an outside voice had spoken to him, presenting one convincing argument after another, and he stood mute, wavering only in the slightest but without any means of contradiction.

He began to feel faint, and with no chair within reach, Nolan perforce had to lower himself to the floor and sit waiting for the lightheadedness to pass. While he waited with his head in his hands and his sweat-coated back stuck against the foot of the desk, his nose caught notes of a loamy odor like that of freshly turned earth. The hour was identical to that of their first evening, when he begged the owner to let them see the room, and in the ensuing silence marked the same scent. Before him the door to the back office stood ajar, granting him view of a window that glowed pink in the evening light and a carpeted floor touched by its rosy radiance. To Nolan's eyes the carpet looked clean, leading him to believe the smell must have come from the soil of a large plant that took up a corner out of sight.

From where he sat, Nolan heard the doorbell ringing, and not long after footsteps came echoing down the narrow hallway. The front door was answered, but he only caught a couple of snatches of the owner's voice.

"I told you no one here is having..." and "Stop bothering us!"

By the time Nolan managed to shift his position to peer at the front door, the owner had slammed it shut and he barely managed to slide himself out of view. It was an instinctive reaction, though Nolan suspected it was futile since he was certain the owner had caught sight of his head disappearing behind the desk. Indeed, he heard her footsteps approaching, and was prickling with anticipation for the moment when she would find him nestling at the foot of the desk. He almost rose up from his hiding spot to cut the suspense short when he heard his wife's voice.

"Who was that?"

"No one," the owner answered coldly. "Just some solicitors."

Nolan guessed the two were passing by the front desk, yet her voice surprised him with its proximity, suggesting that she stood near if not over the front desk, and could easily discover him just by craning her neck to look over the counter.

"Well? What is it?" said Leah after a pause.

Emma in turn said, "I was thinking about—you know—what you told me the other day."

"What about it?"

"Last night I—I heard her crying. I mean I guess I did. I thought it was a dream or that maybe I was hearing things. But then I had a pain—I felt it right here. And I know dreams don't usually come with that kind of pain..."

"That tells you it wasn't a dream," Leah said firmly.

"But—I don't understand... how is it even possible?"

"Do you doubt me, lamb?"

After a brief interlude of consideration, Emma said,

"It's just… remarkable that it happened, I mean it's almost unimaginable that something like that can be done."

The silence on Leah's part was tangible enough that Nolan almost recognized its flavor, recalling the blank stare and pale anger of a PTA mother when she saw she could not cow him into giving her delinquent son a passing grade. When she spoke, Leah's gravelly voice was hard, stripped of her conciliatory good humor. "Do not doubt me, lamb. Do not doubt me or my methods."

"I never said—"

"What you felt yesterday was a taste of things to come. But if you can't trust the process—if you're having second thoughts, tell me now and we will proceed no further with this business."

"Oh no, please—please, Leah—I'm sorry! I never meant to doubt you. Ever since you told me, I couldn't get it out of my head. Last night, it felt so real—and I was sure I was dreaming. But if you're saying it wasn't, I believe you."

"We go all in on this, lamb. All or nothing."

"Of course—that's why we're staying. I talked it out with Nolan and we're staying—"

"Your staying means nothing. You're merely guests here by my invitation."

"You're right, and you've been most generous… Leah, please—I promise you, you won't hear a word from me. I will not doubt. I will not hesitate. Only please, tell me how to go about it—what do I do—I never wanted anything more…" A stifled sob ate up the remainder of the sentence.

Leah's voice grew unexpectedly tender as she said, "It's not how badly you want it, it's how far are you willing to go to have it. Nothing worthwhile comes easy. Do we understand each other, lamb?"

After another wordless interlude during which Nolan heard his wife's sniffing, Emma stammered, "I'd better go and fetch Nolan for dinner."

Nolan drew his knees close and disappeared under the desk while she mounted the steps, and after she had gone, he peeped over the counter to see if Leah was around before rising to his feet and stealing towards the guest bathroom.

After a minute he emerged and ran into Emma coming down the stairs.

"I thought you were upstairs," she said.

"I was—just down the hallway," said Nolan. "I came down for dinner when I suddenly had to go, and I wasn't sure I was going to make it to the bathroom upstairs."

Emma's nose was flushed and her eyes still shone with residual tears, but she pouted a little and reached for his face with a solicitous murmur.

"I'm fine," he said, drawing back, slightly ashamed. "I just need a minute."

The two went and sat in the lobby, taking adjacent seats. From where he sat, Nolan had a side view of the fireplace, and he glimpsed something in the corner there that made him leap to his feet before swiftly collapsing back into his seat lest Emma follow his gaze. In that split second he saw the doll had not only returned but multiplied, and that in that self-same spot was not one or two but a rash of plastic heads of different sizes, clustered like a fungal colony bubbling from the dark corner.

Emma seemed not to notice his start but went on stroking his hand, as if these past few seconds never happened. Nolan observed the faraway look her eyes cast, angled low but not quite down, and the mechanical rhythm her gentle strokes took, maintaining an illusion of presence though her mind wandered down unseen paths.

"You know what I love about this place?" she said abruptly. "Mia was conceived here." She turned to him as she said this, uttering the name without apparent ill-effects. "I know this may sound…" she trailed off, taking refuge in an abstract gesture.

"What?" asked her husband.

Emma stopped waving her hand and sat staring into the empty air, as if waiting for the right words to materialize before her. Then slowly she said, "I like to think she's still here—a part of her, at least, you know?"

Nolan kept his eye on her without answering. It was like watching her sleepwalking towards a high ledge, where a sudden move or the wrong answer might set a catastrophe in motion. What else could he do but remain quiet and listen?

"Honey," she said after a pregnant interval of silence, one that stretched long enough to make her uncertainty tangible; worse yet was how she hesitated still even after breaking it. Then with the delicacy of treading on thin ice, she said, "Do you ever think about Mia?" She looked up and surveyed his eyes. "Do you miss her?"

Nolan dropped his gaze down to the hand she was stroking to see if the color had drained from it too. His lifted gaze took an inward slant as he repeated the question to himself. *Do I miss her? This child of mine that died before she was born?* It would have been easier if he had a chance to meet his daughter—hold her—look into her shiny black eyes and hear all the small sounds she made. But no bond had been forged, no ties cultivated. To miss something was to feel its presence first. How could he miss something that felt almost intangible and not quite real? He'd had the occasional dream in which he had seen his late mother, held her fast, and woke up just before the tears fell. But that was drawn from something that had long taken root. He kept telling himself grief was imminent, that it would hit him in time. It was better than admitting that the baby was hardly on his mind, except where Emma was concerned. Perhaps—as if making up for his apathy—she took the loss harder than he anticipated. Eventually, his lost gaze settled on Emma. Did he miss her? He knew the answer, but it was not one she wanted to hear.

"I can miss her until my heart turns inside out—until my insides spill out," he said, hoping the exaggeration made him sound convincing and somewhat tempered the truth that was to come.

His wife knew it was coming and not bearing to hear it, laid her fingers on his mouth to cut him off. Whatever he said was enough, and perhaps it was better that way—better to end on an empathetic note than risk estranging her.

He took her hand, kissed its palm, then laid it on his cheek and closed his eyes for a few moments.

19

They found Leah waiting for them in the dining room. She bade them sit down, then took her usual seat at the head of the table.

"This is a bona fide feast," said Nolan with arid humor, suspiciously eyeing the generous spread of roast chicken, collard greens, mashed potatoes, and myriads of side dishes.

"We're celebrating your returning health," said Leah, putting on a bright voice that Nolan found more rankling than cologne sprayed to cover a stench. A prudent instinct moved him to return a wan smile, if just to play the fool. A fool he was too, when despite his loathing his mouth began to water at the delectable air that hung in the dining room.

He shifted his focus onto Emma, who twinkled at him across the table and seemed an extension of the owner's dreadful cheer. The notion jolted him with a keen reminder of Leah's sinister influence over Emma. He had a few guesses but not the slightest inkling what the madwoman had told his wife—what she offered in exchange for the promise she extracted from her—except that the thought of not getting it was enough to reduce his wife to tears. Nolan's mouth grew dry at the thought of telling her he had changed his mind and they were to leave soon. Could he even hope to convince her, or would he have to resort to leave this place short of dragging her bodily away? The idea alone nearly broke his heart, more so when her quiet sobs were still fresh in his mind. Even if the situation justified the means, how would he manage to go through with it without his car or even a cab standing by, ready to carry them away?

While he went on ruminating, he mechanically passed his plate to be filled then just as absently set it before him, failing to register the food until his wife called his attention to it.

"Aren't you going to eat?"

Nolan found his plate heaped up with chicken, greens, and mash generously coated with gravy. "I don't think I can have that just yet," he said, pushing back his plate.

"Nonsense," said Leah. "You're well enough to eat like a spring bear. Go on—try it," she said, enticing him with a morel mushroom that had the savor of butter. "I know you're hungry. I'll feed you well."

Nolan's gaze darted from the offered mushroom to Leah's face before searching the table and seizing a sealed packet of butter as the least likely unadulterated food item on the table.

"There, I'm eating. I'm eating," he said, scooping the softened butter out with two fingers and proceeding to eat it. And over Emma's ensuing protest, Leah said, "Let him be. Come breakfast time, he'll probably be ravenous enough to eat for two." She winked and cackled.

The remark earned her an angry glare, which Leah answered with a smile. "Oh, now Mr. grumpy puss, don't look so mad." She made to pinch Nolan's face though he leaned out of reach. "Why don't you have a small bite of this, and I'll tell you what a little birdie told me?"

"I'm not in the mood for games," grumbled Nolan, who had half a mind to take the butter and leave the table had he not noticed the apprehensive glance Emma cast in Leah's direction. There was a shade of surprised guilt in that look, subtle enough to make Nolan question his perception.

"Look how pale he is!" cried the owner, clicking her tongue.

Nolan ignored her and went on observing his wife, trying to discern what her transient expression had meant. A touch near his mouth made him flinch, and he saw it was the same mushroom Leah had speared with her fork and was offering him to eat. Again he refused, and Leah sighed and with downcast eyes retracted her fork, eating the bite meant for Nolan.

"I guess he doesn't want to know then."

"Know what?" asked Nolan, not expecting a response from the owner and so repeating the question to his wife, who likewise avoided his inquiry.

"You know, I can't help but marvel at the flavor in these little ones," said Leah, lifting a fork to consider the a cluster of velvet shank mushrooms. "I always say things taste better when you feed them. Any fool can grow tomatoes in a bit of dirt, and they'll come out all red and full, but they won't taste like much—"

"You're full of it."

"They won't taste like much," Leah continued, "because you have to feed the soil. That's nature's way. I have fed my garden to feed you, so we can have this feast. From earth and to earth, from feeding to being fed on—" she rhapsodized, carrying a mushroom-bearing fork to Nolan's mouth—"on and on, and so on and so forth... So let it be."

Nolan looked at her, spared the fork a glance, then without moving his head, turned an inquisitive side-look to Emma, staring under eyebrows that were lowered in an uncertain frown. His wife beamed on him, almost encouraging him, and her smile remained even when Leah pushed her fork into his slack mouth, withdrew it, and thumbed the corner of his mouth to wipe off a smear of grease.

"She did something to you, didn't she?" was Nolan's unspoken conclusion. It was enough to make him spit the morsel out of his mouth, if only he didn't suspect the process would be repeated in exchange for their damned secret. It occurred to him then that he might have left the table and waited for his wife to tell him in the privacy of their room what he now dreaded to hear—only it was because the news seemed so significant (and a matter of amusement to their host) that all other considerations were lost in the shadow it cast.

He closed his mouth as he looked back to Leah, chewed and swallowed.

"Well?" said Nolan when seconds passed after he had swallowed without anyone speaking.

Leah held his gaze, and he almost excepted her to make him eat another bite. Instead she set down her fork and took a sip from her glass before speaking.

"Your wife decided to move here and run the place with me."

The reveal was so unlike anything he expected that he found himself wading through perplexity, through scant relief, and then back into a sense of foreboding until the full import finally dawned on him.

"You can't be serious," he said, his voice suddenly so hoarse that it came out in a whisper.

Emma met him with a smile brighter than its predecessor, anticipating a giddy reaction now that her delightful secret was out. But her joy dimmed considerably when she saw he was not smiling over the happy news.

"It's what we wanted, wasn't it?" she asked through a lingering ruin of a smile. "This was our retirement dream. Only I managed to bring us a step closer."

Her husband began shaking his head long before she concluded her sentence. "We don't want this. You never even—" He stopped with supreme effort to modulate his rising voice. "Did it even occur to you to talk it over with me first?"

"What's there to talk over?" she chuckled. "We both like the place, it's ten times bigger than our apartment."

The lack of logic baffled him more than the announcement itself. "Are we talking about running the place or living in it!"

"The whole point is to do both," she slowly explained, brightening in the glow of inner visions. "We'll make it work, I know we will."

Nolan remained impervious to her enthusiasm—the same enthusiasm he had long yearned to rekindle—knowing the notion had been in her head for the past two days, yet recognizing the part Leah played in twisting them to their current form.

"You want us to move here?" he asked, struggling to follow her plan.

"We always said we'd get a bigger place eventually."

He began to answer but caught himself before he let slip the bigger house was conditional, meant to accommodate their growing family. Likely Emma knew it too, though he doubted she steered the conversation in this direction by design. At any rate, she evidently found his delayed answer troubling, suspecting perhaps that he was about to go back on his promise. She set her mouth and met his gaze, almost challenging him to say something. "Well, I found us a place," said she when he failed to speak. "I want to settle here."

At this, Leah laid her gaunt hand on Emma's with a gesture that to Nolan's eyes appeared closer to appropriation than solidarity. The theatrics were enough to make Nolan roll his eyes but he held back, knowing any show of hostility could weaken his position. Just the same he remarked, "If the idea of indentured service appeals to you..."

"That's not how it is," argued Emma.

"No? What is she offering, then? A partnership?"

He expected his wife to answer, or else be taken aback over a blindspot. Instead she continued to regard him with eyebrows gathered in a plaintive scowl. A subtle flush crept up her face, which alongside her prolonged silence served as a warning sign.

"I thought you'd be happy for me—or that you'd understand," she said, and it did not escape Nolan's notice that Leah gave her an encouraging squeeze of the hand, as though the two of them were united in facing an adversary.

He in turn sighed. "Could we at least discuss this when we go back home?" he said, seeing the futility of carrying a normal conversation while the two of them were bent on turning it into an emotional minefield.

"This is home," said Emma and then flinched when her husband struck the table. His face was clouded with color, and he was fixing the owner with a glare.

"I don't know what your game is, but you stay the hell away from her."

Leah raised her eyebrows, and perhaps affected to widen her eyes, though her heavy lashes hindered the result. "Am I meant to take this as a warning shot? Is that hand going to strike me next?"

Nolan looked taken aback by the accusation. "What are you talking about?"

"We wait on him hand and foot for a day or two and now he thinks he's master of the house," the owner continued in an aside to Emma. "I say we ignore him until he learns to behave himself."

At first instance Nolan hardly heeded the threat, and went as far as to scoff at their childish strategy. Such tactics were not unfamiliar to a teacher who's encountered them in the form of a difficult student challenging his authority at every turn. Such students were draining to deal with and the episodes were liable to sour his day whenever they occurred, but often enough the student was sent to the principal's office or made to sit through detention while Nolan took a long stroll home, and the aftermath of such incidents hardly if ever crossed the barrier of sleep into the next day. Much as he cared for his students passing their class, some issues were beyond his control, and he was all too glad to leave them up to the parents or school counselor.

But now he could hardly retain the same cool and detached temper he employed in such cases, more so when the two ladies began discussing future plans regarding the bed and breakfast—or rather Leah was making plans while Emma listened close and gave the occasional nod. The longer Nolan stared at the two, the more he felt himself on the verge of a breakdown. Just what did the madwoman promise his wife?

"Emma, for God's sake!" he cried, desperate to break that last vestige of resistance and make her look his way. In a last ditch effort, he almost upended the table but found the unit too heavy and himself too weak to do more than give it a shove that rattled the dinnerware. Then it came to him with inward mortification that he was reverting to behaving like a child in order to solve the situation. It was enough to make him sit with inarticulate anger, until the first words that fell from his mouth was a half-pled demand directed at Leah.

"No more, please! No more!"

Leah continued to ignore him as she stared ahead, took an untroubled sip of her glass, then set it down. "I think it's time you went to bed, Mr. May."

Though Nolan continued to regard her, a creeping numbness caused his eyes to open a little wider in a moment of recognition before his lids sank down. This time, there was no tablecloth to catch on the way down, and he suffered the crash with his senses still registering the sharp crack of his head hitting the floor. Sight and hearing were the last to go, so that he had time to get a darkening glimpse of the underside of the table, and hear Leah's voice floating somewhere above.

"To the triumphant irruption of the plant in us!"

20

Nolan tossed and turned but sleep would not come—no position offered comfort, no contortion carried him into oblivion, far from the laughing ruckus. Through closed eyes he saw the dark bedroom, knew they occupied a corner beyond his line of sight, heard the two recite a few lines from a song, their voices rising in harmony for a moment, promising to complete the wretched rhyme before one of them fell into peals of laughter and dragged the other down.

He wanted to tell them to be quiet, but he was half-asleep, tangled in a dream state, and when he finally managed to open his eyes, the room was empty and still.

Under the yellow bathroom light Nolan found the tiled floor strewn with strands of long black hair, enough to make him step back before entering, his full bladder urging him on. He aligned himself in front of the toilet and managed to get a steady stream going. Halfway through it, a dull ache dilated through his right flank, an invisible hand closing over his kidney endeavoring to wring more fluid out of him. The pain lingered sometime after he was done, clouding the air with an unusual odor, beckoning him to glance down and expect blood or froth. He discovered neither but found a layer of black hair coating the water.

His hand, reaching for the flush handle, remained suspended for an immeasurable time then pushed the lever, sending the black hair eddying down, while from the tiled floor the drain hole made a horrible sucking sound.

Nolan left the bathroom, sending wisps of hair flying like insects. Outside his room, the hallway was just as black as the bedroom, and in the heart of it he stood listening. There was little to hear besides the self-contained hush of pulse and his own breathing, then a thin shriek faintly sounded in the distance. Again it came, shrill yet brief, calling him to it. He moved to follow, his legs slow to obey.

From the gaping black something flew at him. He caught a flash of white wings spread against the dark before it struck his face. A whooping chaos of flapping wings smote his cheeks and ears. He tucked his head between raised shoulders and held up his hands, his crossed arms taking the worst of its scratches before the bird retreated and flew in another direction. Still Nolan kept his eyes shut until he heard a dull thump and the beating clap of wings failing, and he understood without seeing that the bird must have crashed into a wall.

The space was lit by the moon, and underfoot the soft soil sank a little, telling him that he had veered off the paved path. The bus stop was half a mile away—a short walk, as long as his direction was true.

Back in the room, Leah came to check on him. If he lay still, he might fool her into thinking he was asleep in bed, and not on his way to catching the next bus. If he could embark, and let it take him as far away as it would go, he might make a clean break before returning to fetch Emma. But Leah was not convinced: she closed in on the bed, becoming more eminent by degrees, growing taller and taller, until her sable head eclipsed the ceiling lights and cast a long shadow to make him lose his path. And so he was back in his room.

That room, that room, that damned room.

Even in the pitch black he saw the wall of flowers—roses borne by upward spiraling vines, each bloom peaking skywards, each with an eye in its center. His bare feet left muddy prints on the bare floor as he approached the wall and the many eyes moving to track him from within the folding petals. One by one he poked the eye at the heart of each rose, intending to put them out only to discover a flat surface of painted paper and the hard wall behind it.

But he was not wrong, he knew what he sought, and what he sought was found when he pressed into the heart of one rose, and felt the petals flinch and close like lids around his finger.

Slowly, gently, he pulled the finger back and stared into the eye now closed to leave the rose with a blank center. He raised his hand, tentatively extended an unsteady finger, and pressed again. The thin layer resisted but slightly, yielding with a sigh of escaped air as his finger poked through the wallpaper.

At the table they served him a plate of soft potatoes and went on talking, as if they didn't know he knew. But he remembered the cry, thin as the rip of fabric, and he remembered, too, what he saw beyond the wall for flowers, when he stood on his toes and craned his neck to look through the gouged hole, and then turned to find his bed blighted with the smooth heads of dolls, as though the damp sheets had sprouted them through the bedding. Under his back they bent and collapsed but never went flat, and so made sleep almost impossible.

In the bright dining room, his eyes rolled with every slow turn of his head, trying to keep up with the ever-tilting surroundings. He listened while he pretended to eat, and pretended to eat while he listened. If he could go another day without eating, with only a few drinks from the bathroom faucet, maybe his head would clear. And so he must keep his head down and now and then drop the fork, and when his wife retrieved it he would drop the spoon, and then the fork again.

"She would turn on him and grab him like this," said Leah, laying her long-fingered hands on Emma's shoulders. "Just like that. They would be mating, and he would be holding her by the waist. But she would still turn on him—first getting a taste, then sinking her mandibles into his neck, chewing clean through. All the while, his decapitated body was still attached and providing—oh, yes!—and she got more from him than she would have with his head attached. He would have held back, but she would take it all. So there she stood, holding his head and munching on it while taking all his seed—stowing it for her need—and he watching her take and eat, getting a good view of himself before everything went dark."

A key on the dresser, thought Nolan, striving to recall what he saw through the hole in the wall. The memory was small and he was liable to lose it as he almost did now if he didn't stop to remind himself. Under the dining table, one dirt smeared toe scratched the ankle of his other foot. His car key on her dresser. If he could get it, if he could get it...

Key on the dresser, *key on her dresser*, he thought over and over, now and then putting a finger to his pursed lips to keep the words from spilling out, ignoring their talk and looks while he went on mashing his food with a fork.

21

The house was semi-dark, suffused in the sanguine gloam that reddened the cloudy air and lent a ruddy hue to every shadow. His head felt clearer though a persistent haze marred his vision, so that even with his glasses on, everything was seen through a fine mist.

Though he passed through a torrent of dreams, Nolan had managed to keep the hole in the wall at the forefront of his mind, clutching it for fear it would wash away in the throes of a troubled sleep.

"Key on the dresser, key on the dresser," he muttered to himself as he rose from bed and unsteadily stole towards the rose-strewn wallpaper, now reddened by the dusk. *Car key on the dresser*, his mind added to better affix the image, augmenting it with details like a wrinkled brown leather fob and a copy of his apartment key.

Though he had yet to settle whether his car had indeed been towed or whether Leah had something to do with its disappearance, the fact she had his key did not surprise him. He took what he saw through the hole in the wall for solid fact—that is, until he reached the same wall and discovered that none of the blossoms bore an eye in the center of its folds. To verify this, he stuck a finger in each one, seeking the hole in the wall, undiscouraged from his purpose until his efforts proved futile, and he turned away convinced that the conniving petals had closed their lids to hide them, and that he was better off investigating the room himself. Bathed in red gloom, the doorway of his room stood open, beckoning him to the task. He gave a brief and dreamy smile in answer.

The back of his neck pricked with sweat while he stood bracketed by the doorframe, listening for voices or movements about the house. All was quiet, with that hush peculiar to a house after the electricity went out. Only the sound of his soft tread reached his ear, and at first he found scant comfort in hearing something outside of himself. A mere few steps was all it took to get to the room next door, into which the hole in the wall must have looked. The door was locked, but enough sense was left in Nolan to advise him to try the lobby for the room keys.

On a landing halfway down the stairs was a window that showed the trees outside, their branches still as a painting, and the soon-to-fall leaves were just as unmoving, as if the house itself had fallen into a pocket out of time or space. Nolan thumped the side of his head with the heel of his hand. Nothing changed, except he seemed to have unstuck the notion of finding the room keys and so continued down the stairs.

There were no keys behind the unmanned desk, and for the first time Nolan stared at the ever-gaping back office door, this time not hesitating to step through. A fetid smell struck him just before he crossed the threshold and turned left on instinct to find whatever caused the stench and discovered a white cluster covering the wall there.

In the red light that streamed through the window and gave everything a florid wash, Nolan saw the eruption of colorless mushrooms that covered the wall, and from a glance seemed to have sprouted from there. But Nolan could see—could indeed not help but see—the faint humanoid outline making up this dense forest of pale mushrooms. Yet no trace of a body was visible. From crown to sole, upward curving stalks lifted layers of caps and crowded over the flesh from which they grew and fed. The figure half-sat, half-reclined against the wall, so that the head and shoulders were propped up while the rest stretched out on the floor.

Nolan himself now slumped against the door, which supported him more than his splayed legs could. He covered his open mouth, almost as if to keep himself from screaming, though for the moment the only sounds he was capable of were the hitched breaths with which he tried and failed to fill his lungs. It was just as well, for when he finally managed to draw the dank air, a wave of heavy nausea struck him and he turned away and crawled out of the office.

Time ceased while he remained huddled under the front desk, staring unperceiving over his knees, his hands so weak and wet with sweat that he had trouble keeping them clasped under his bent legs.

The terrible sight had obliterated all thoughts save those born out of instinct. He had to leave—he had to get up and leave now—never mind his car keys... Where's Emma? Oh, God! Where's Emma? He had to find her and run! They had to get away. Why wouldn't his legs move? He had to unclasp his hands. But he was afraid of letting go. His thighs pressed against his stomach was the only thing that kept him from getting sick, and he feared falling into a faint from weakness.

With returning thoughts his senses soon followed, and Nolan began to hear a cry like that of an infant right above him. The noise was familiar yet so unexpected he had to hear it again and again.

One shrill cry followed another, almost but not quite convincing him that an infant lay on the front desk. Something was off about the cries, an initiative quality which nonetheless compelled Nolan to come out of hiding and see for himself. His nausea had ebbed in the interval, but he was hardly aware of the fact as he crept out and put his hands on top of the desk to raise himself.

On his knees, Nolan's head was on level with the desktop but not the raised counter, on top of which lay a swaddled bundle. Though it sat a few inches above him, he saw it move, languidly squirming as if trying to break free from its confining wraps but was powerless to do so. With its struggle came the fussing cries that left Nolan with little doubt of their source.

Before he had time to do anything, the bundle was snatched off the counter and carried away. While the receding cries traveled up the stairs, Nolan went back to cowering under the desk, more on instinct than from any known reason. Though the cries had long faded, they still echoed in his mind, until it dawned on him that there was an infant upstairs—an infant who in all likelihood was abducted for some unknown purpose.

Nolan's unblinking eyes mechanically traveled towards the back office doorway before he scrambled out of hiding, possessed by a sudden instinct to rescue the baby.

22

There was no sound to guide Nolan, and so he followed his hunch and made his way down the long hallway to the master bedroom, all the while ignoring the possibility of confronting Leah. No doubt the woman was dangerous, but caught off-guard she might not have time to try anything. He barely had time to think of Emma and her whereabouts, except to imagine how—once she laid her eyes on the kidnapped infant—it would be far easier to persuade her to abandon this place and leave with him.

Nolan found the master bedroom door ajar and lurched through, intending to catch the owner unawares and half-expecting to find the infant laid on the bed or sofa there.

Like the rest of the house, a cloudy red gloom had suffused the space, and like the rest of the house, every surface was crowded with a myriad of robust plants. His glancing search discovered the population of baby dolls sitting amongst them. A closer scrutiny revealed the dolls themselves served more than a decorative purpose—long leaves poked through their mouths or else thrust out of their scalped heads. A larger specimen even had vines weeping out of its eye sockets.

Nolan, still dazed by his surroundings, failed to note the whiff of sulfur before an unexpected shove landed him on the spring mattress. He lay supine, his poor eyesight affording little more than an impression of the figure towering over him. In a heartbeat, Leah climbed on top, straddling his waist and using her knees to pin his arms down. Without use of his arms, Nolan bucked and fought in vain to throw her off, while she had both hands free and were now sweeping them over his face. She took away his glasses to facilitate this, and in a voice that she seemed to draw deep from within her she bade him close his eyes and sleep.

"You're just having a bad dream," she told him over and over.

To his horror, Nolan felt his eyes half-close and a heaviness steal over him, replacing the frantic energy he needed to throw her off. The frightened noise issuing from his throat were sounds he believed had long been abandoned—left behind with his playground days, namely that one incident in which a group of bigger kids had held him down and threatened to feed him a worm. Nolan's glasses had been knocked aside then, and he defiantly called the older kids bluff up until the moment in which his eyes focused on a glossy pink worm, dirt crusted and writhing between pinched fingers, inches away from his face.

It was happening again, and the tears in his eyes stood testament to the fact, though it was Leah's hands which now continually hovered close with their downward sweep.

"I'll have you when the fight's left your body," she promised.

Nolan all but dislocated his shoulder wrenching one arm free. He felt a tearing down his side and abdomen, both of which were barely registered in his haste to plant one palm flat against her torso. It was then that he felt the long, stringy hair thickly coating the rock-ribbed chest, and realized her dress was gone.

Whether by accident or design, the pressure from her knee abated, allowing Nolan to slip his other arm out, and presently he closed both hands about her neck.

Horror piled on horror when for a split second he pondered what he was about to do. Despite what he knew, despite what was happening, his retaliation felt disproportionately violent to the offense, and the innate pacifism robbed him of his resolve.

Leah knew this and mocked him. His hands seemed to petrify, and the throat between them reverberated as she cackled with significant delight that turned his insides to water and made it impossible for him to force his hands to tighten their grip.

While Nolan held her at bay, he began calling out for Emma, wildly hoping the threat of being discovered would force her to relent.

When it happened, he couldn't say, but Emma did appear by the bed. In the semi-dark and without his glasses, Nolan more sensed than saw the hazy figure out of the corner of his eyes. But who else would it be?

"Call someone! Call the police!" he cried. He caught a shift of movement in the peripheries of his vision and heard running steps, giving him a measure of hope that help was on the way so long as he kept his assailant at bay…

Leah grabbed Nolan by the throat and on her part did not hesitate to apply enough pressure to make him release her and claw at the hands choking him. With an iron-grip like that, she might have easily snapped his neck. She instead constricted her hold, hunching over him until he blacked out.

Nolan came to at the odd sensation of his feet dropping and striking the floor, but in his disoriented state did not understand that he was being dragged down the banister-less stairs until he was flung over the side and landed on a heap of earth. Then a potent spell of dizziness swept him away, and the last thing he heard was a reiteration of Leah's promise. "I'll have you yet..."

23

Nolan stood at the edge of an open grave with his hands folded before him. Emma chose not to come, or rather could not come. So he alone attended the private ceremony. While he waited he thought of the little body about to be lowered there and felt heartless when the thought failed to move him. He liked to think he was being strong for his wife's sake, though it bothered him to imagine what the few attendants thought of his dry eyes and stony face. To remedy this, he stared down into the grass-lined hole—dug too wide and too deep for a small casket. Then with dawning alarm, he began to hear faint cries issuing from the black depths, and without pausing to consider why they were burying a child who was evidently drawing enough breath to cry, Nolan dove headlong down and landed hard on the turned soil.

His head gave a dull throb that made him heavy-eyed and at the same time contended with the barbed pain about his throat.

Just as his lids sank down, he again heard the infant cries coming from somewhere above. Clumps of dirt adhered to his cheek as he jolted up, suddenly remembering the stolen baby. He had a moment to wonder whether Emma managed to run off or call for help before looking around, trying to locate where he was, inclined at first to believe he was somewhere outside. His blurred sight translated little of his dim surroundings, though from the threads of light filtering through shuttered or tape-covered small windows, he guessed he was in the basement or some subterranean section of the house. There was the septic stench poisoning the air, though it was the sensation of something writhing out of the damp soil and onto the back of his hand that drove Nolan to his feet.

Meanwhile the infant cries continued to resonate somewhere overhead, their maddening recurrence convincing Nolan they weren't mere phantoms as he half-suspected. As before, it did not escape him that there was something off about the cries, but having limited experience with babies and even less capacity to dwell on such a small matter, he knew little what to make of it except to believe the baby must be starved or hurt in some way.

Nolan winced at his burning throat as he trudged on through unidentifiable mounds that variably smelled like coffee dregs and urine-soaked earth. When his cold feet finally found a concrete step, Nolan raised his head towards what he presumed were a flight of stairs leading up to a landing if not a closed door. His upward squinting eyes softened into a wide look of dread as he again remembered his wife, fearing the worst yet unable to think it. There was no banister to guide him up the stairs, but the uncertainty of mounting steps in the semi-dark did not in the least slow him.

At the top of the stairs, the closed door was left unlocked, and through it Nolan found himself in a room both large and crowded, overhung with a pungent smell. Gone was the reddish twilight glow, and the house stood in reigning darkness.

Nolan bumped his way through what he believed was a store room—now clutching a thin metal post of a shelving unit, now accidentally swiping a jar that shattered on the tile floor—until his hovering fingers caught a wooden object with sliding handles, one of which he pulled to discover a small knife, and realized he was in the kitchen. The handle remained in his grip, knowing well he needed something to fend Leah off—or more realistically something to brandish and make her think twice about attacking him. Chances were she was still somewhere in the house, and the few dozens of steps that separated him from escape seemed to stretch out in his semi-blind state. And yet he still needed to find Emma, or at least make sure she managed to flee the house. Then there was the infant, whose distant wails now came at irregular intervals...

The sound was Nolan's sole means of finding his way out of the kitchen, playing hot and cold with it and following it till he finally reached a door that opened to a short hallway.

Past the hallway, Nolan looked about the unlit lobby area with uncertain recognition, wondering if a moving figure hid itself amongst the crowding silhouettes of plants and furniture, and it was there in that relatively open space that he heard the first notes of Emma's laughter and felt a cold snap in the pit of his stomach.

He stood frozen at the foot of the stairs while like lightening a line of unthinkable scenarios ran through his mind to account for her laugh.

Slowly—almost reluctantly—he climbed the steps, clutching the banister for support and growing more fearful when her laughter flowed into gibbering. His fear-addled mind never thought to connect the infant cries with his wife—not even when Nolan reached the open doorway of Room Three and with rounded eyes beheld the lamp-lit room where Emma stood by the bed, cradling the swaddled bundle, her delighted laughs mixed with its thin cries.

However wide his eyes stood open, Nolan could not uncloud the murky outline of his wife swaying the bawling infant in her arms any more than fathom why she was calling it by their dead daughter's name. Without thinking—without even meaning to—Nolan crossed the room to grab Emma's arm, wrenching it harder than he meant to. The wriggling blanket slipped through her arms and fell to the floor. One horror was replaced with another as the dropped bundle stirred, and some unseen form scurried away with injured squeals.

Nolan caught Emma just as she was about to dive after it.

"No more! For God's sake, Emma, no more!" he wanted to shout but only managed a few raspy croaks that were drowned out by her heart-rending wails. His hands went from clutching her arms to holding her face as he bade her look at him, but her eyes remained shut, rumpled in agony like the rest of her features.

"Look at me!" he begged, on the verge of collapsing. She went on senselessly heaving a series of hitched breaths, until through some small mercy she finally broke into anguished sobs. Nolan still held her when they sank to the floor and remained kneeling, half-propped against the side of the bed. A sense of unreality enveloped him, never quite resolving into a dream from which he could wake up, though it kept his frayed and tenuous sanity from snapping altogether. When he tried to hold Emma closer, he realized one of his hands still had the knife from the kitchen and put it down lest his wife broke into another fit of frenzy.

While his splay-fingered hands secured her head and back, Nolan's mind entered a zone of dead calm as he simultaneously considered the near and far future: they would have to walk to a bus station; he might need to check her in a hospital; he needed to fetch his wallet to cover the bus fees; could he leave Emma here while he ran down to phone for help or would he have to take her downstairs with him? Would they be better off separating? None of it made sense. All he knew for certain was that they he had to move, yet his legs did not obey him in unbending to that purpose.

"Dear Mia," his wife coaxingly murmured against his shoulder. "Where's Mia?"

"She's gone, Emma," he answered without hesitation. "She's gone—long-gone."

Emma lifted her head to look at him, and her proximity let him see her unfocused gaze which had a note of defiance in it.

"She's here," said Emma. "This is where she began. This is her home. She's still here."

Her husband tenderly smoothed her hair down and gently spoke as if trying to reason with a willful child. "She's at peace now. Let her sleep."

When she said nothing to repudiate this, Nolan slowly rose to his feet and persuaded Emma to do the same. She refused and pulled her hands away, and the gesture told him what he could not read in her face.

The persistent pain in his throat kept him from arguing. He let her stay while he went to fetch his wallet, then again tried to pull her up.

"I'm staying here," she said, not meeting his gaze.

"Emma, for the love of—! We have to go now!"

"Fine, go then!" she countered. "I'm staying here."

The rising anger in him almost reached its volcanic peak, and he thought the kindest thing—in the interest of both their welfares—would be to drag Emma to her feet and force her to walk. But she remained obstinately rooted to her spot, as though her folded legs were welded to the floor.

Finally he let her go, and felt for the first time in his life the urge to slap her, if just to wake her up. Had she not seen what transpired in the master bedroom?

His anger somewhat abated when it crossed his mind then that she might not have been in the master bedroom—that in his desperation he had only imagined she was there. Should he tell her, then? In her current state the effort seemed as futile as getting her to move. The wisest—if not only—course of action was to leave her here and lock the door behind him while he descended to the front desk to call the police.

As he turned to see to it, he heard Emma calling him; something in her tone made him stop and turn—just a backward glance. But a backward glance was all it took.

From an unseen angle, the shovel head met his, and swiftly brought him down.

24

His head gave a twitch as one eyelid fluttered halfway into opening, briefly showing a slit of white before sinking down. After some time had passed, both eyes opened again, and when Nolan saw the cloudy view of a white ceiling, and rolled his eyes half an inch to the corner where the flowery walls met the blank expanse, he gave an involuntary cry that translated into a nasal groan—too weak to sunder his sealed lips, too faint to be acknowledged by the two women who were out of view but whose voices betrayed their presence.

"We must act quick while she is yet lingering. His essence is key. Otherwise, it won't work."

"But how do we—?"

"There are two ways to go about it. If the regular method doesn't do it, we'll try it the other way."

"What's the other way?"

Silence; and then: "Go to the kitchen and fetch me a baster…"

25

Winter set in early that year, and the first guests of the re-opened bed and breakfast were a couple who had car trouble on the way to a nearby county but found they were a short trek away from the establishment. There weren't enough rooms to lodge many guests, but the ladies running the place agreed they could accommodate about five or six—one guest in the small room, a couple in another, and a small family of three to squeeze in the slightly larger room.

Room Three, separated from the other guest rooms by a long corridor, remained occupied for the time being, and towards it Emma presently made her way, bearing a breakfast tray of toast and boiled eggs. She opened the door and beamed on her husband, who sat in bed and seemed to prefer to stare out the window than acknowledge her presence. What he saw there without his glasses was unlikely to transfix him to the point of ignoring her, and Emma had to console herself with the fact that at least his health was improving. His hollowed out face was beginning to fill out, and this morning, the cheek he presented her showed hints of a high color. But it was only natural since he sat in bed all day, and lately the trays she carried bore empty plates, indicating signs of a returning appetite.

Emma bade her husband 'Good Morning' and tried to get into his line of view while she set up the bed table, but he went on staring through her at the frosted window.

"I'm sorry breakfast is late," she said, pretending to have hit upon the reason why he was being sullen. "We've had guests coming in earlier than expected. Their room wasn't ready, but we served them coffee in the lobby and they seem to like it there, what with the fire going and all." She placed his morning pill conspicuously next to the tall glass of orange juice and feigned to arrange the bed covers while keeping watch out of the corner of her eye to make sure he took it. She had a feeling that if she hovered over her husband and waited for him to take his medication, he might grow suspicious or stubborn and refuse to take it. Thankfully, he cooperated and took the pill, tossing it back almost automatically and chasing it with a sip from his glass.

The medicine was meant to rejuvenate him, and personal observations satisfied Emma that it was doing just that. She was far too occupied to notice the pill disappearing down Nolan's pajama top sleeve where it sat until he got up and went into the bathroom. He was thankful he at least had that measure of privacy, and with more guests arriving, their watch was growing more lax, and they took it for granted that he would remain in Room Three. Then again where would he go without a car, his wallet, his glasses—his wife? She wanted to stay here, so stay here they shall.

He glanced at her now, while she wasn't looking and assumed he too had his attention set elsewhere. Even with blurred vision, he saw her form, saw the bend of her head as she looked down and placed her hands on her stomach, trying to measure the imperceptible swell with the tender air of secret hopes. The gesture was transient, and he was careful to glance away at the slightest shift before she caught him.

He too had plans and secret hopes, and under the bed cover he caressed the forgotten kitchen knife that now lay over his leg. That night, while they sat on the floor leaning against the bed, he had slipped the knife between mattress and bed frame, and had only recently remembered it after he had stopped taking his medications and the heavy stupor that had settled over his mind began to lift. His memory returned bit by bit, and in the long idle hours he relived with painful clarity everything that befell him between that night and the present. Drop by drop the details fell into place, until finally he remembered the knife, and discovering it was still there was like finding a canteen of water in a dry wasteland. This morning, he experimented with taking it out and tucking it under cover, resting the sharp object over his pajama-clad thigh, secretly running a finger over the flat side and feeling a slight shiver from the proximity of the blade.

"Nolan," he heard Emma say, and the sound of his name almost surprised Nolan into slicing his thumb. He took his hand out, realizing it must look odd to have one hand in his lap and the other tucked under the covers.

She surprised him again by sitting on the bed at his side, unintentionally jostling the knife so that it slid down and came to rest against his inner thigh.

"Nolan," she said again, searching his face yet failing to notice the brief drain of color there or the averted look of alarm. She took his hands as if to hold his attention before continuing. "Nolan, I want to say that I forgive you."

This forced him to look at her.

"Do you remember that night?" she went on, dropping her gaze to the hands she held and which she now stroked. "I saw you and Leah—in her room. You were—it was—" She squeezed his hands as if caught in the throes of a painful episode. "What I mean to say is what's past is past. And that I forgive you."

Emma closed this with a pat on his hand to demonstrate her goodwill. "At least we're happy now. And we'll grow together—with a growing family. It's everything we wanted."

When she freed his hands and stood up to leave, Nolan remained caught in a daze that made him insensible to his wife's movements. The spell was short-lived, and he called her just as she reached the door.

He might have imagined it, but he saw her back stiffen as he asked her to come close, and guessed she likely dreaded re-opening an unpleasant subject. Only she was wrong, so very wrong.

Again he asked her to come close when she stood by the bed and did not move. Something in his calm voice told her it would be a bad idea to disobey, so she inched a little closer. But the proximity she offered was not enough, and it was his turn to take her hand and compel her to sit down as she had done not a minute ago. He then placed a hand on the back of her head, as if intending to grab a handful of hair, if just to keep her from slipping away.

Having come this far it was his turn to ask her if she was indeed in the master bedroom, if she saw what she saw and did nothing—worse than nothing, given the conclusion she drew.

"Do you forgive Leah too?" he wanted to ask, but felt he could not pose the question without something inside him snapping. He only needed one hand to hold his wife, and the other slipped under the cover.

Without warning, her hands flew up and held his face. She made a small sound that was either a sob or a suppressed laugh.

"This is everything we wanted, isn't it? It's just us here in this sweet little place."

Her face was an inch or two beyond clear vision, and Nolan could not tell whether it was a smile he saw or a grimace. He likewise could not say whether she somehow divined his intention or was blissfully ignorant. For an interminable minute he continued to study her face, trying to reach an answer. Then the hand at the back of her head grew a fraction gentler, while the other hand slipped out from under the cover to press her hand to his cheek, as if to imprint the shape of her palm in his mind as much as his face, however faint.

"It's everything," he answered, cupping her cheek, gently stroking its curve with his thumb.

By then she seemed almost as reluctant to leave as he was to let her go, but there were guests waiting and a room to prepare for them. She came down with her empty tray to refresh their coffee or else remove the cups and ask them if they needed anything.

The couple sat by the window, and the wife complained of a draft that made her coffee grow cold. Her grumblings were interrupted by an audible thud that came from above.

The three of them heard it and looked up, though only Emma knew it came from Room Three. She excused herself just as her guest was about to expand on her grievances, and the lady was loud enough to be heard by Leah, who was manning the front desk.

"I'll have a look," said the owner, intercepting Emma. "You go and see to our guests."

Emma obeyed and returned with apologies and offers to appease the unhappy woman, whose husband contrived to hide himself behind an unfolded newspaper. Again, the woman's string of complaints was cut short by a crash coming from above, far louder than its predecessor. Again Emma excused herself and went upstairs to see.

"That's it! We're leaving," said the wife, picking up her handbag and heading in the direction of the guests bathroom, which the husband took to mean she would need a minute or three before they returned to the car. He welcomed the break however brief it was and went back to his paper. His enjoyment was marred by the scream that tore through the upper floor and jolted him into looking up, when promptly another sound drew his attention to the view outside the window.

There he saw a blond man in pale blue pajamas rising from a mound of snow into which he had evidently landed. The man had his back to the window, and without turning or stopping to brush the snow off, he staggered away and disappeared from view.